BABYMOUSE AND FRIENDS*

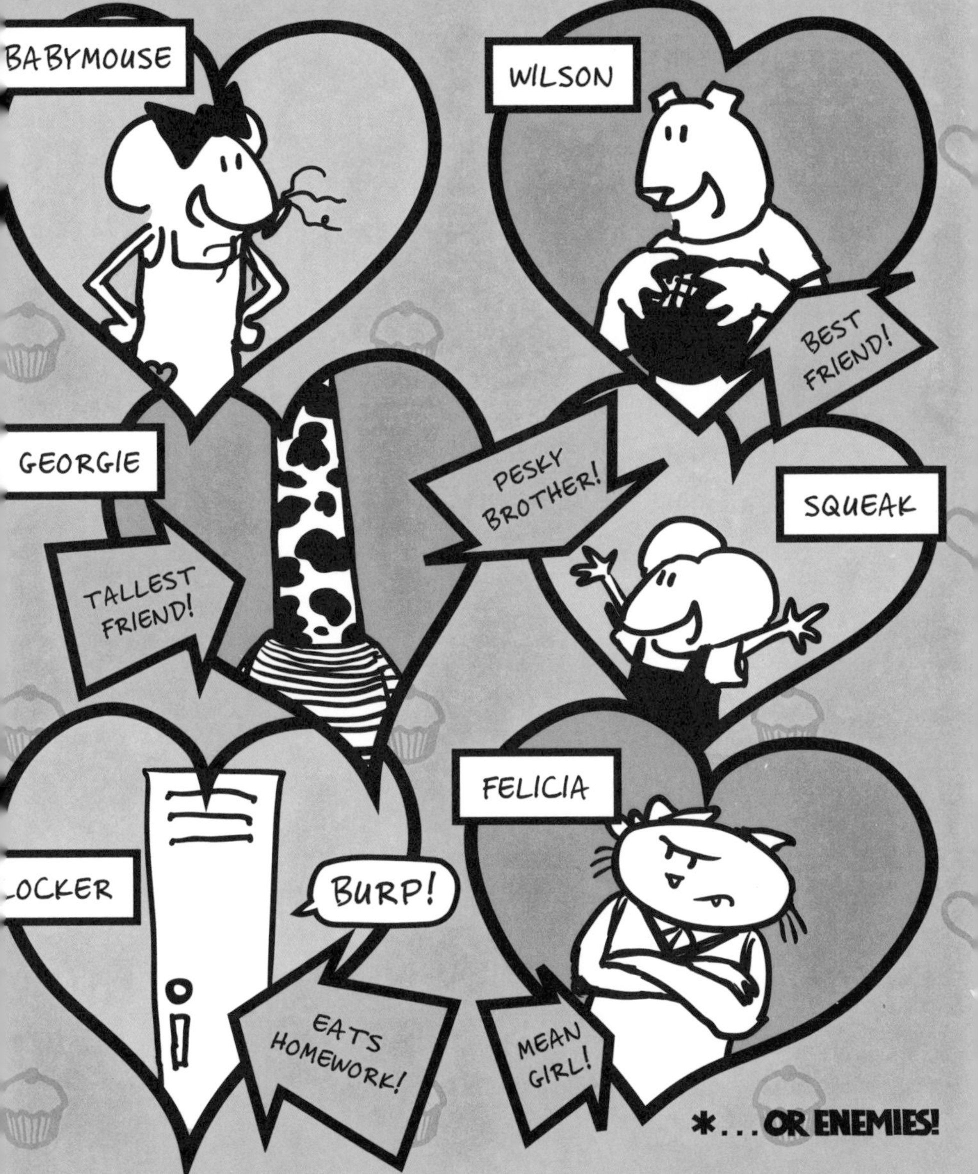
BABYMOUSE
WILSON
BEST FRIEND!
GEORGIE
TALLEST FRIEND!
PESKY BROTHER!
SQUEAK
LOCKER
BURP!
EATS HOMEWORK!
FELICIA
MEAN GIRL!

*. . . OR ENEMIES!

Be sure to read **ALL** the **BABYMOUSE** books:

#1 BABYMOUSE: Queen of the World!
#2 BABYMOUSE: Our Hero
#3 BABYMOUSE: Beach Babe
#4 BABYMOUSE: Rock Star
#5 BABYMOUSE: Heartbreaker
#6 CAMP BABYMOUSE
#7 BABYMOUSE: Skater Girl
#8 BABYMOUSE: Puppy Love
#9 BABYMOUSE: Monster Mash
#10 BABYMOUSE: The Musical
#11 BABYMOUSE: Dragonslayer
#12 BABYMOUSE: Burns Rubber
#13 BABYMOUSE: Cupcake Tycoon
#14 BABYMOUSE: Mad Scientist
#15 A Very BABYMOUSE Christmas
#16 BABYMOUSE for President
#17 Extreme BABYMOUSE
#18 Happy Birthday, BABYMOUSE

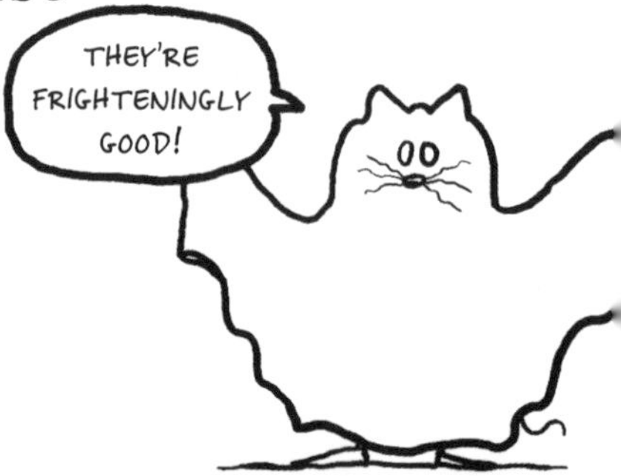
THEY'RE FRIGHTENINGLY GOOD!

BABYMOUSE

MONSTER MASH

R.I.P.

BY JENNIFER L. HOLM & MATTHEW HOLM

RANDOM HOUSE NEW YORK

Copyright © 2008 by Jennifer Holm and Matthew Holm

All rights reserved.
Published in the United States by Random House Children's Books,
a division of Random House LLC, a Penguin Random House Company, New York.

Random House and the colophon are registered trademarks of Random House LLC.

Visit us on the Web!
randomhouse.com/kids
Babymouse.com

Educators and librarians, for a variety of teaching tools, visit us at
RHTeachersLibrarians.com

Library of Congress Cataloging-in-Publication Data
Holm, Jennifer L.
Babymouse : monster mash / by Jennifer L. Holm & Matthew Holm. — 1st ed.
    p. cm.
Summary: A graphic novel following the Halloween adventures of Babymouse, an
imaginative young mouse.
ISBN 978-0-375-84387-7 (trade) — ISBN 978-0-375-93789-7 (lib. bdg.)
1. Graphic novels. [1. Graphic novels. 2. Halloween—Fiction. 3. Mice—Fiction.]
I. Holm, Matthew. II. Title.
PZ7.7.H65Bam 2008 [Fic] 2008008433

MANUFACTURED IN MALAYSIA   20 19 18 17 16 15 14 13 12 11

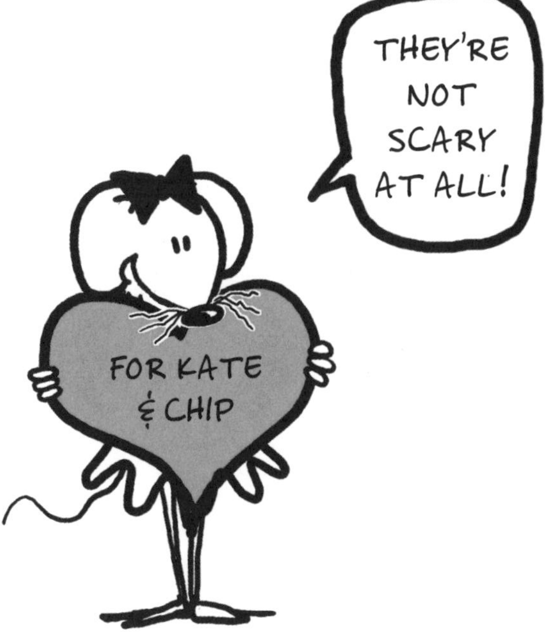
THEY'RE NOT SCARY AT ALL!
FOR KATE & CHIP

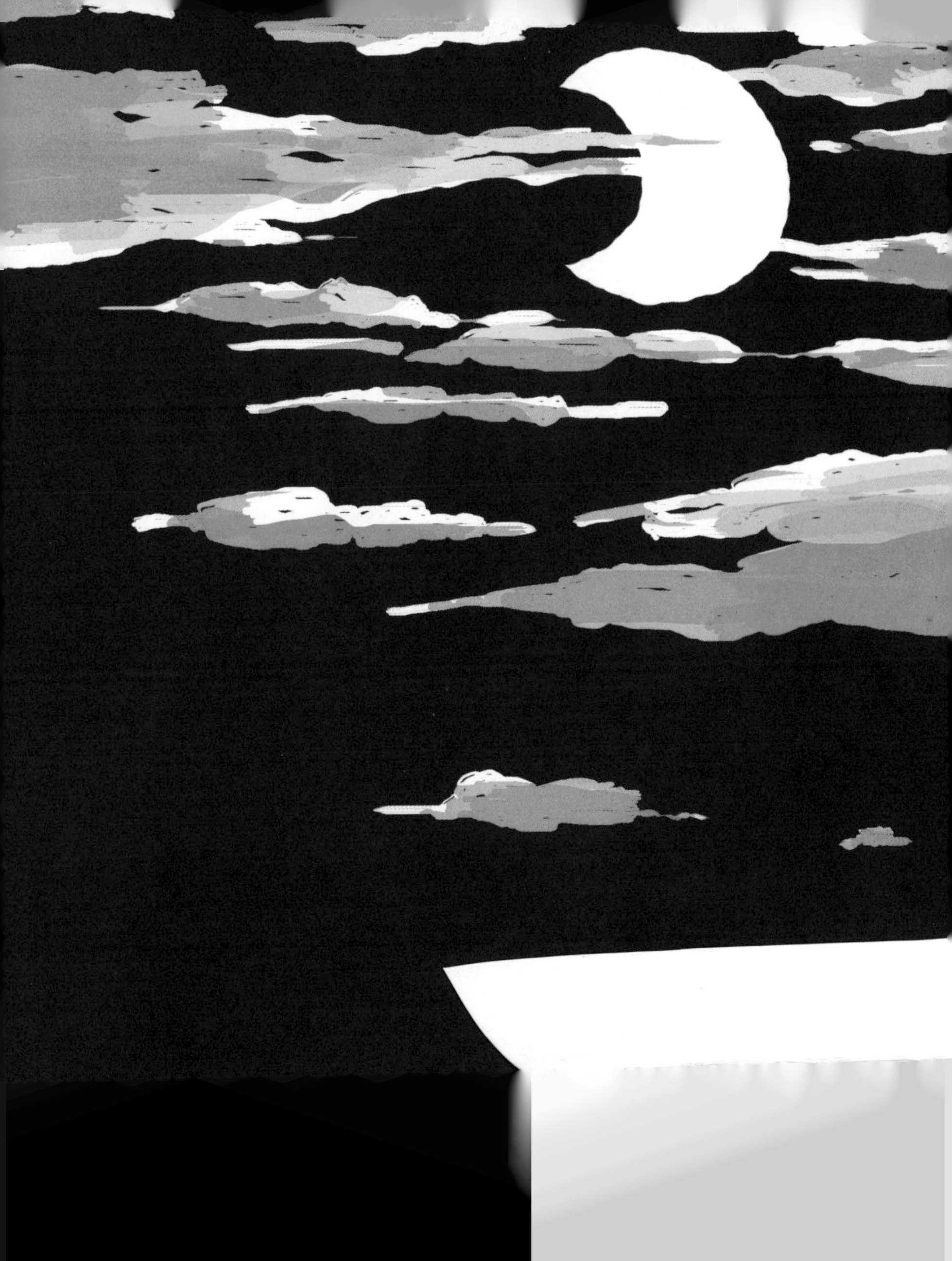

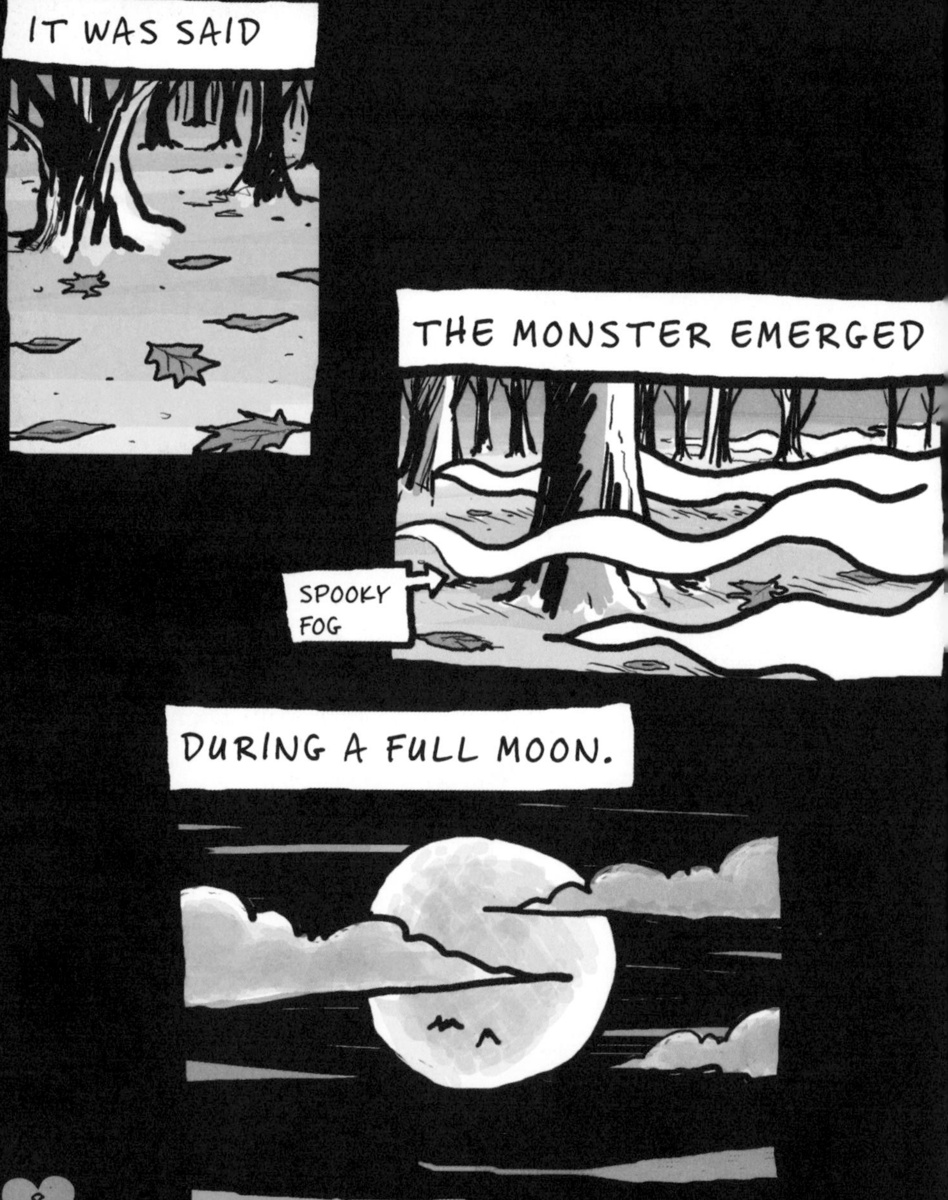
IT WAS SAID
THE MONSTER EMERGED
SPOOKY FOG
DURING A FULL MOON.

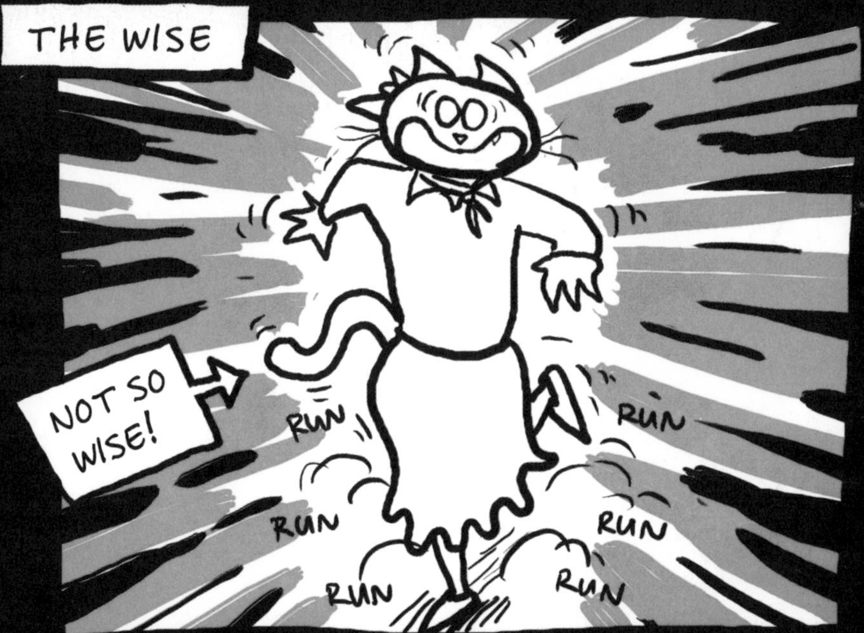
THE WISE
NOT SO WISE!
RUN
RUN
RUN
RUN
RUN
RUN

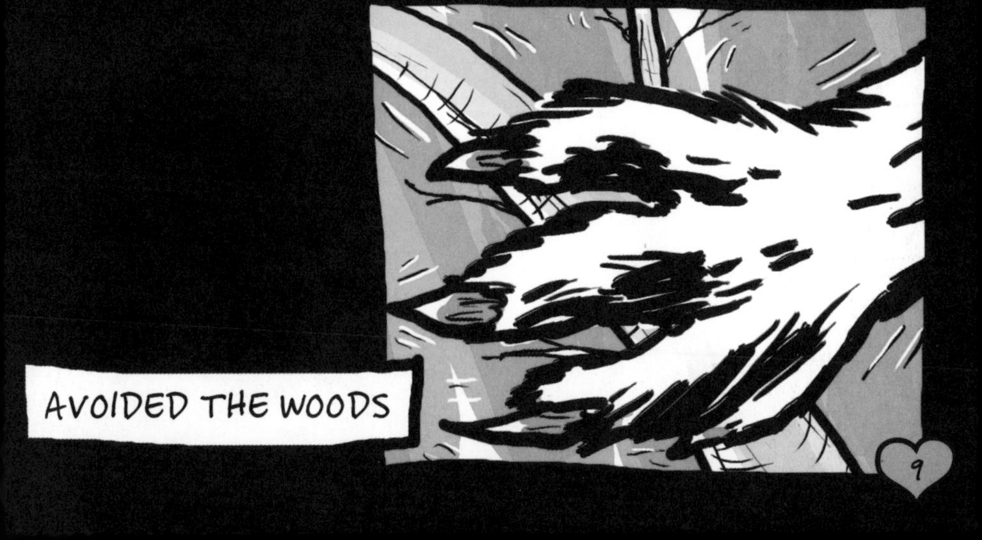
AVOIDED THE WOODS

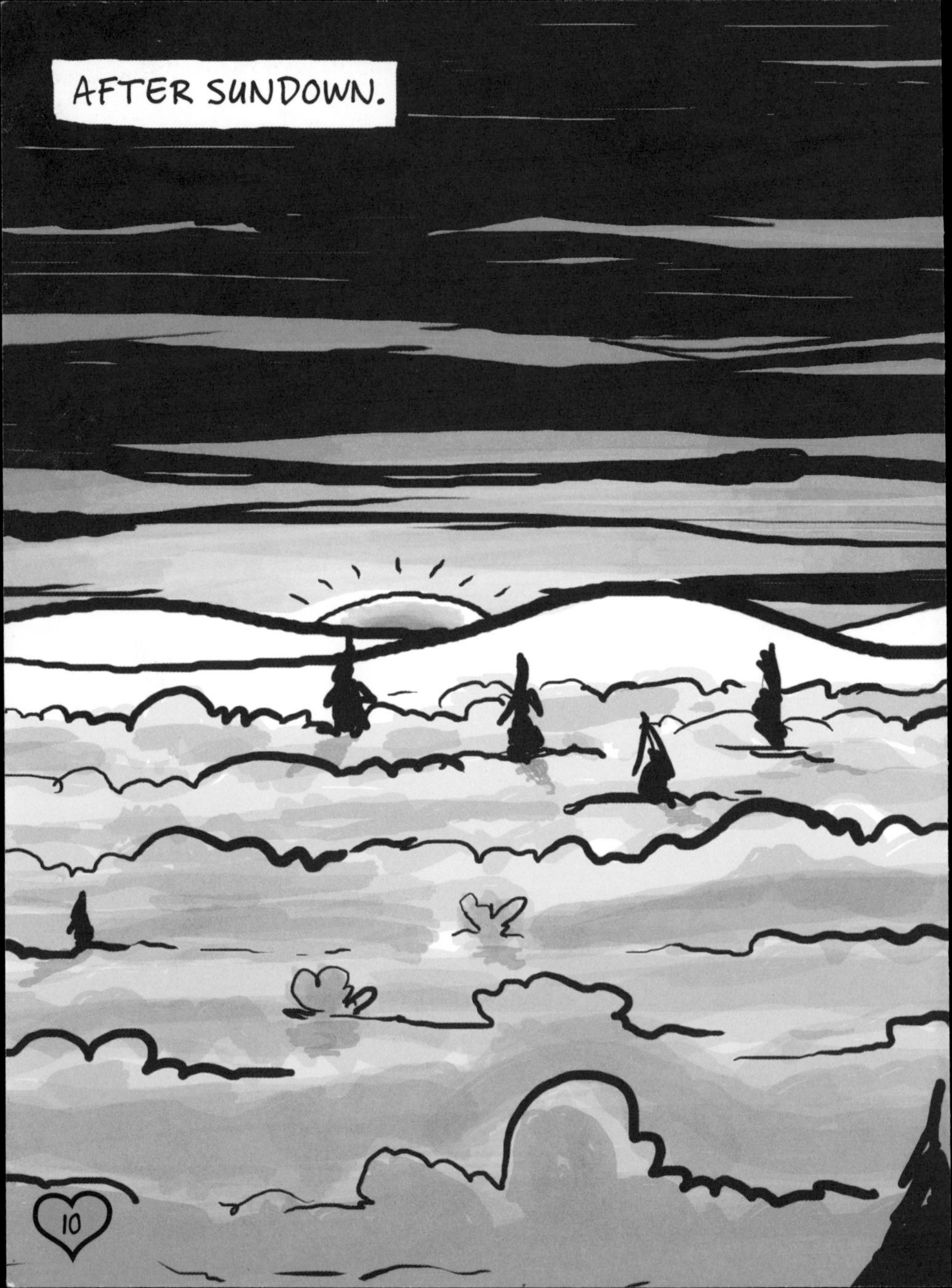
AFTER SUNDOWN.

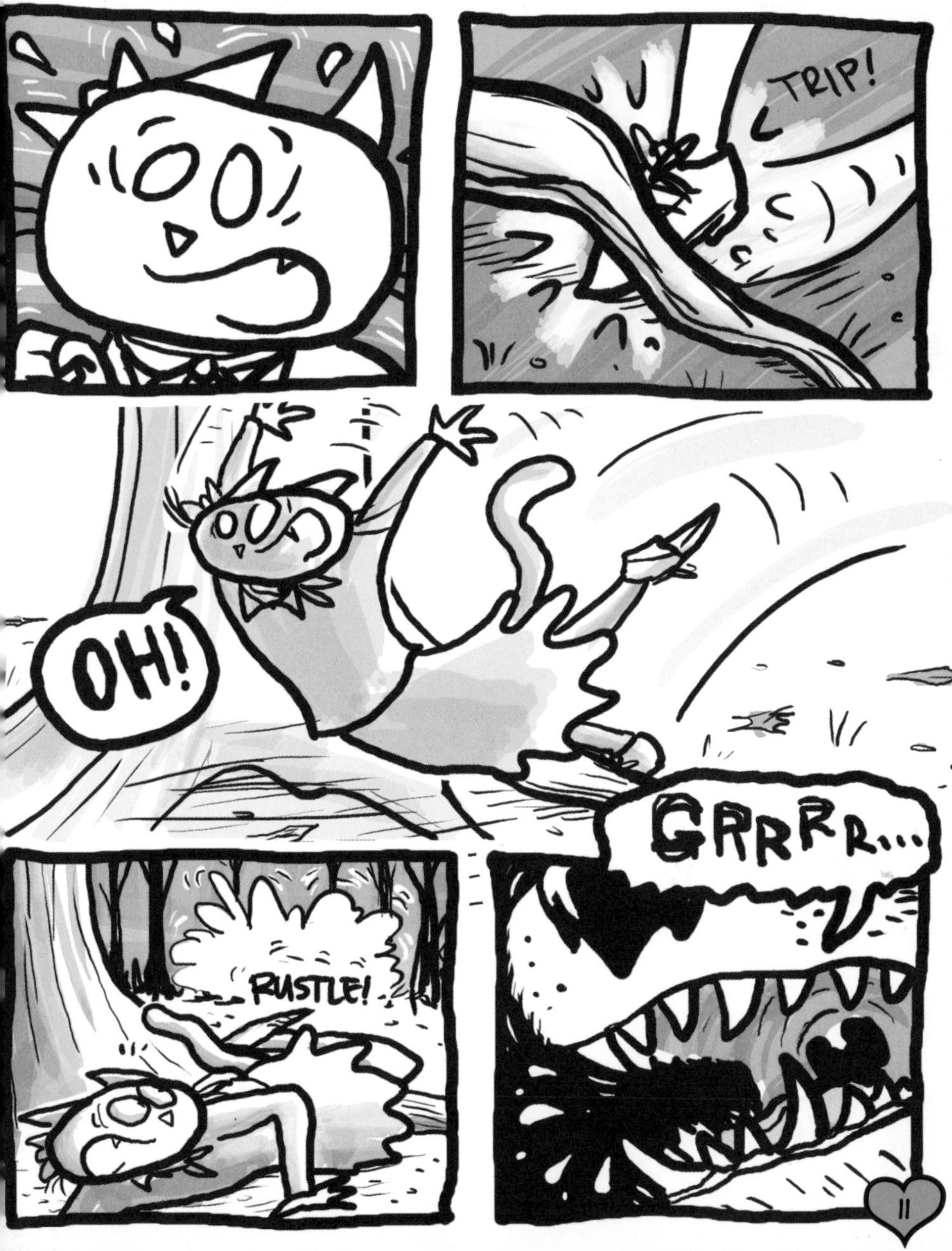
TRIP!
OH!
GRRRR...
RUSTLE!

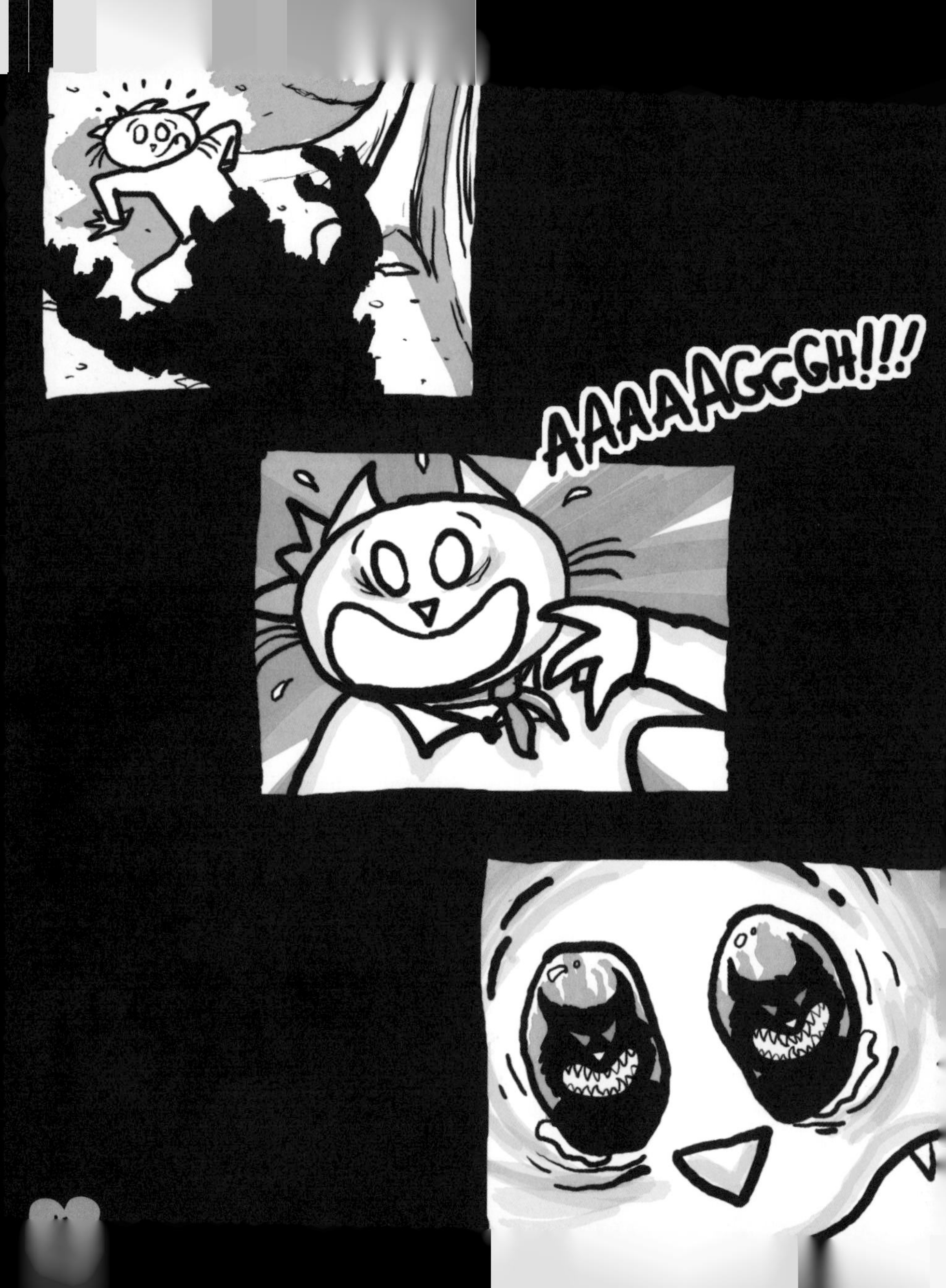
AAAAAGGGH!!!

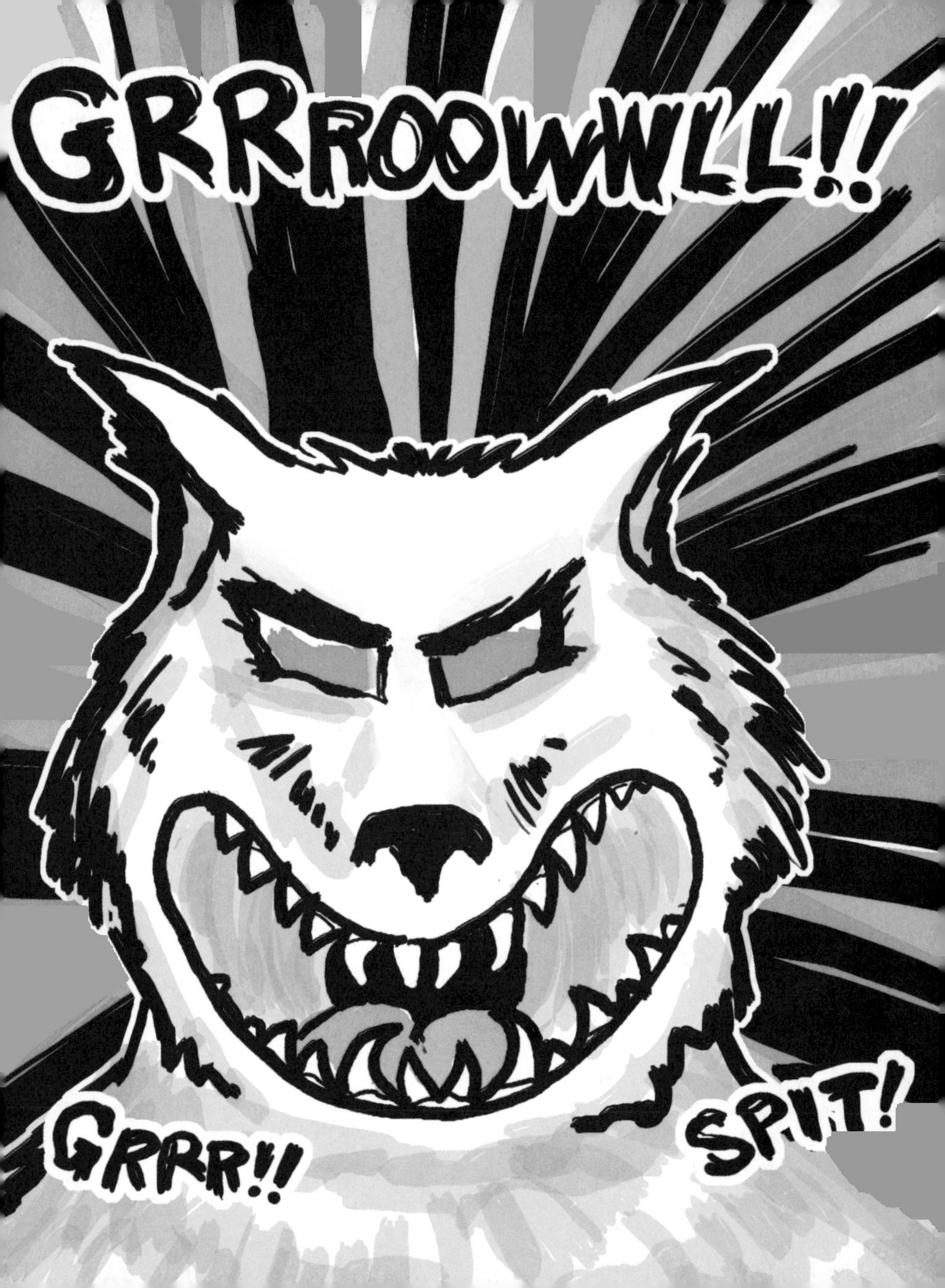
GRRROOWWLL!!
GRRR!!
SPIT!

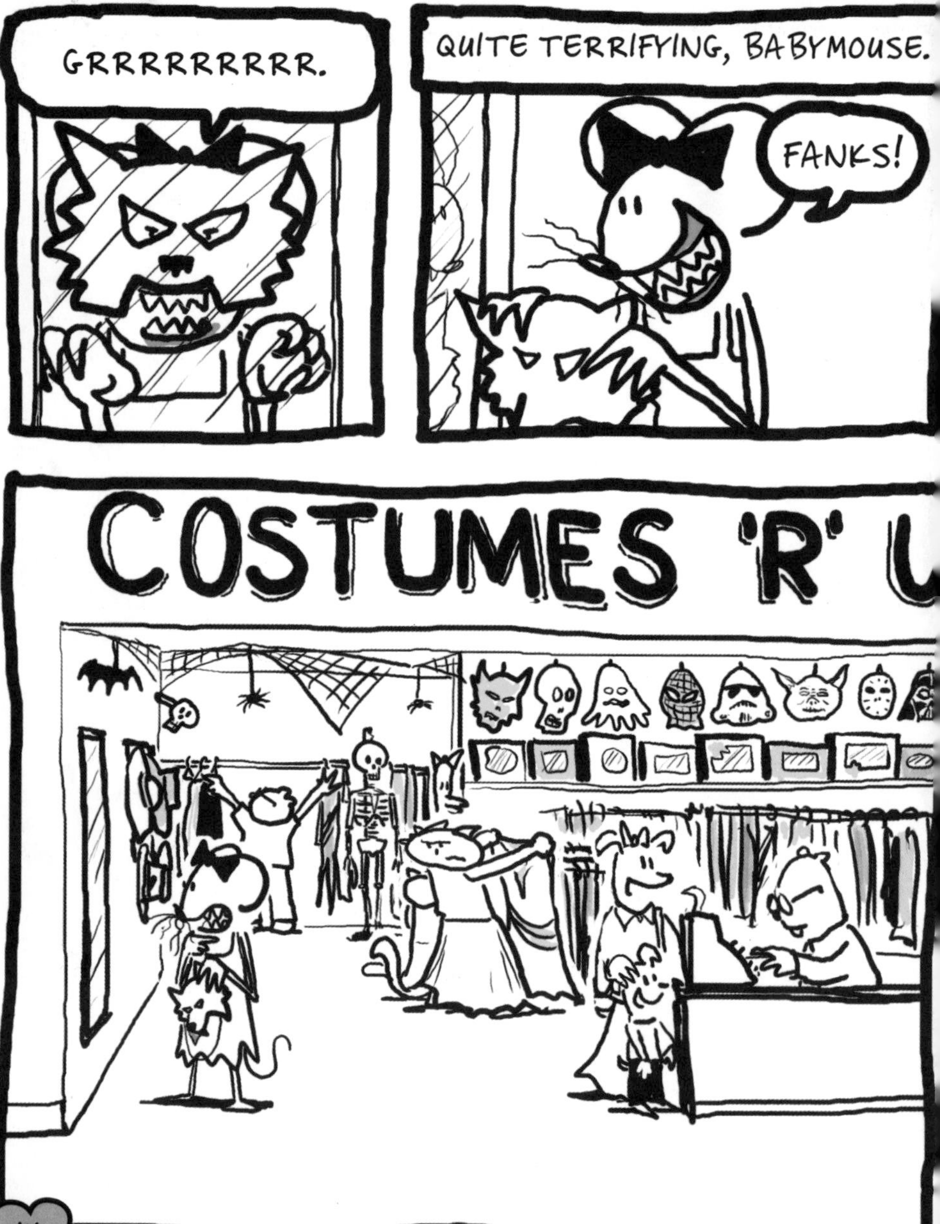

GRRRRRRRRRR.
QUITE TERRIFYING, BABYMOUSE.
FANKS!
COSTUMES 'R' U

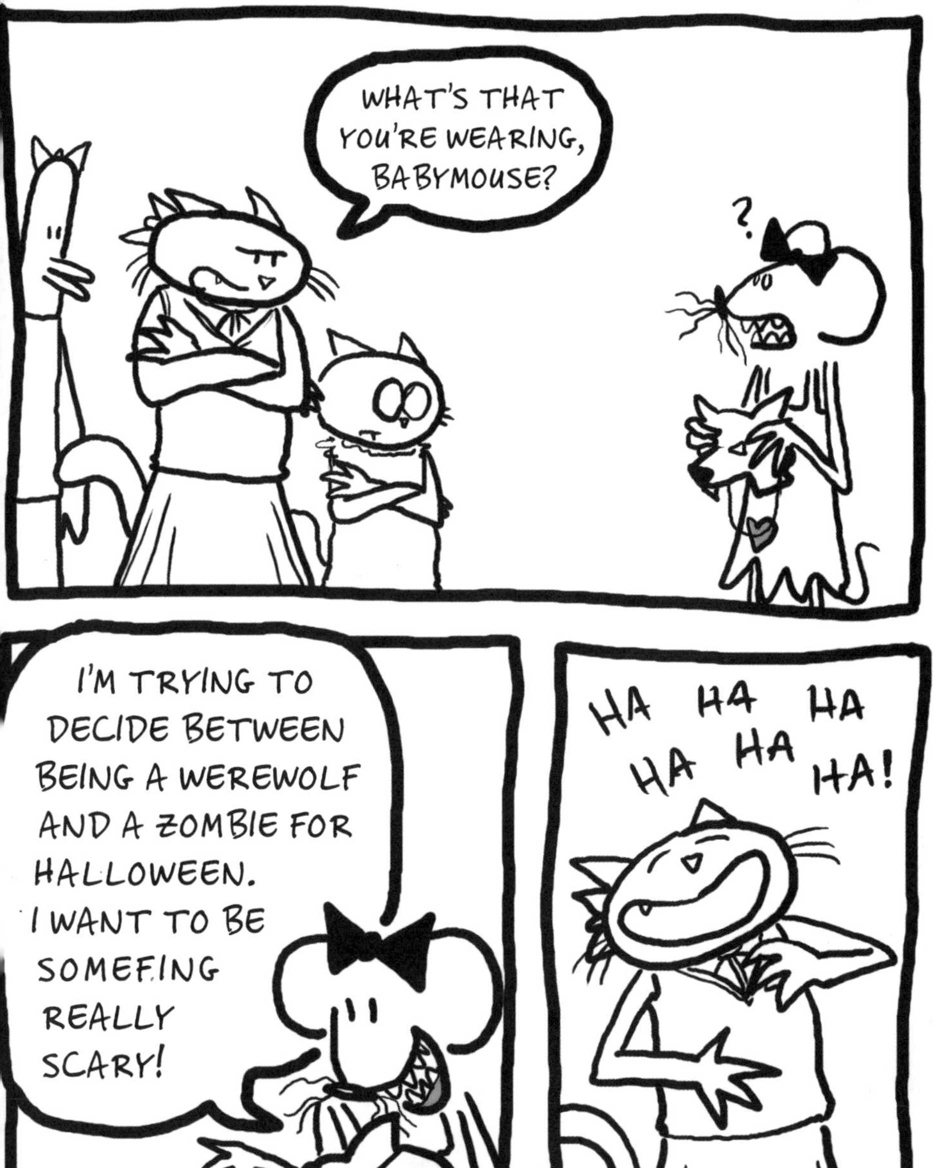
WHAT'S THAT YOU'RE WEARING, BABYMOUSE?
?
I'M TRYING TO DECIDE BETWEEN BEING A WEREWOLF AND A ZOMBIE FOR HALLOWEEN. I WANT TO BE SOMEFING REALLY SCARY!
HA HA HA HA HA HA!

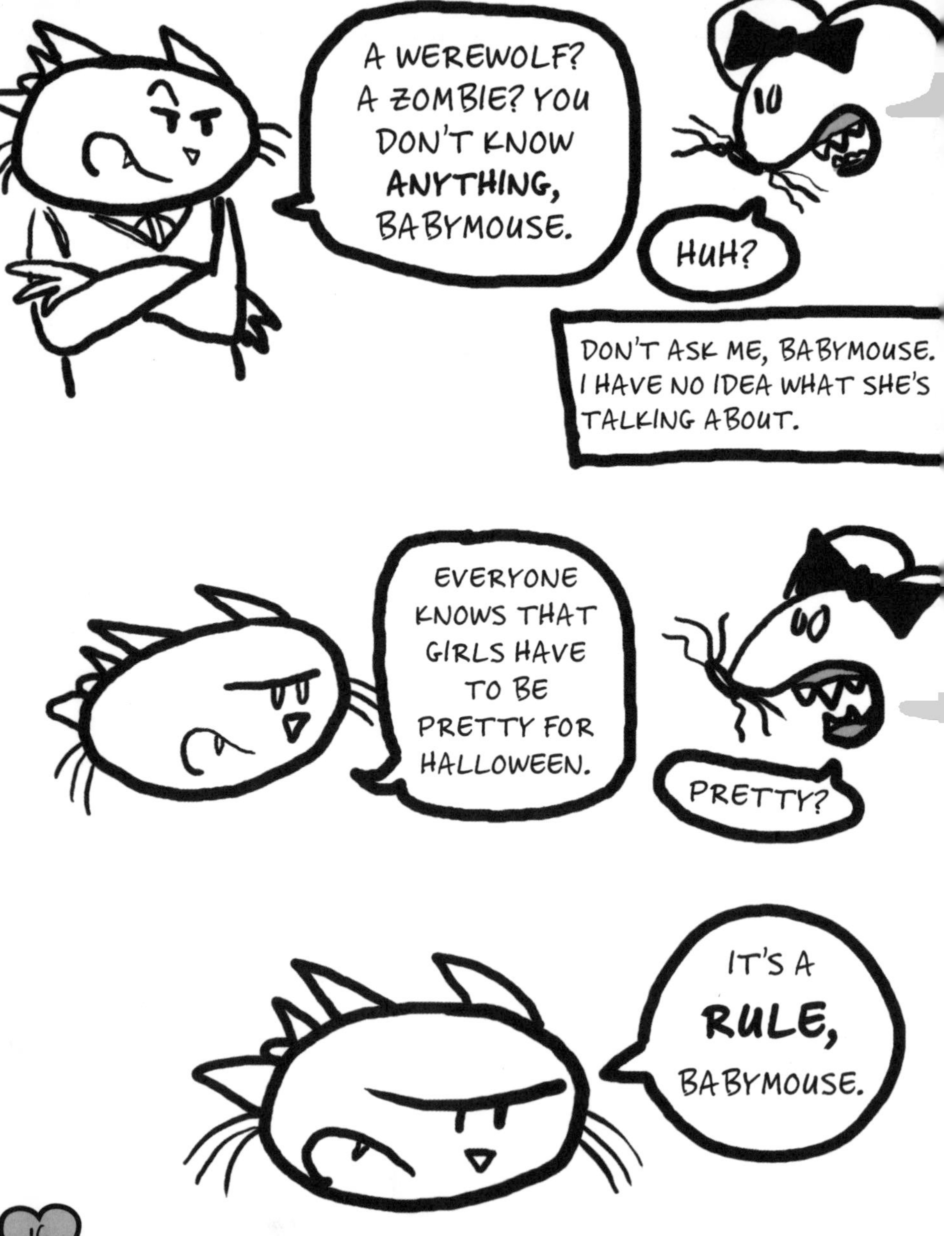

A WEREWOLF? A ZOMBIE? YOU DON'T KNOW **ANYTHING,** BABYMOUSE.
HUH?
DON'T ASK ME, BABYMOUSE. I HAVE NO IDEA WHAT SHE'S TALKING ABOUT.
EVERYONE KNOWS THAT GIRLS HAVE TO BE PRETTY FOR HALLOWEEN.
PRETTY?
IT'S A **RULE,** BABYMOUSE.

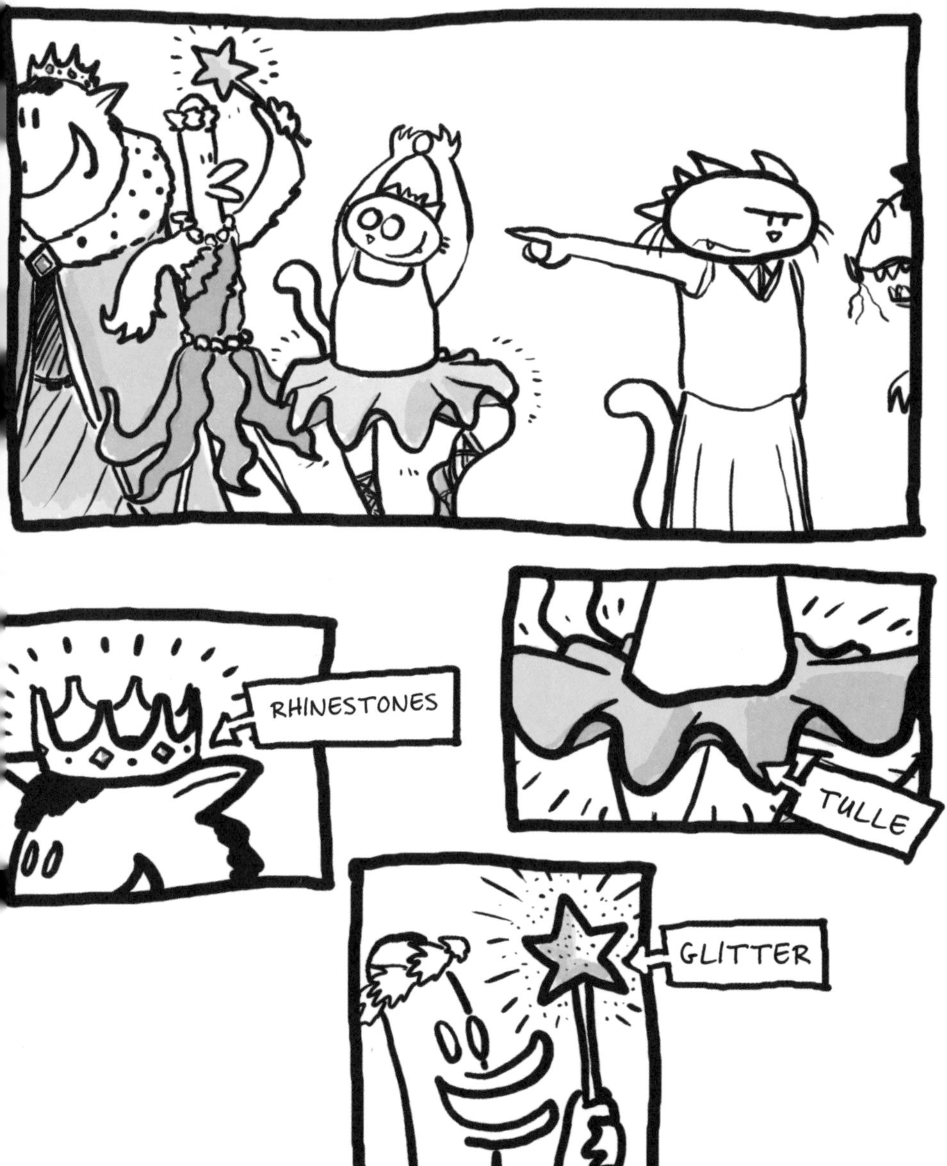
RHINESTONES
TULLE
GLITTER

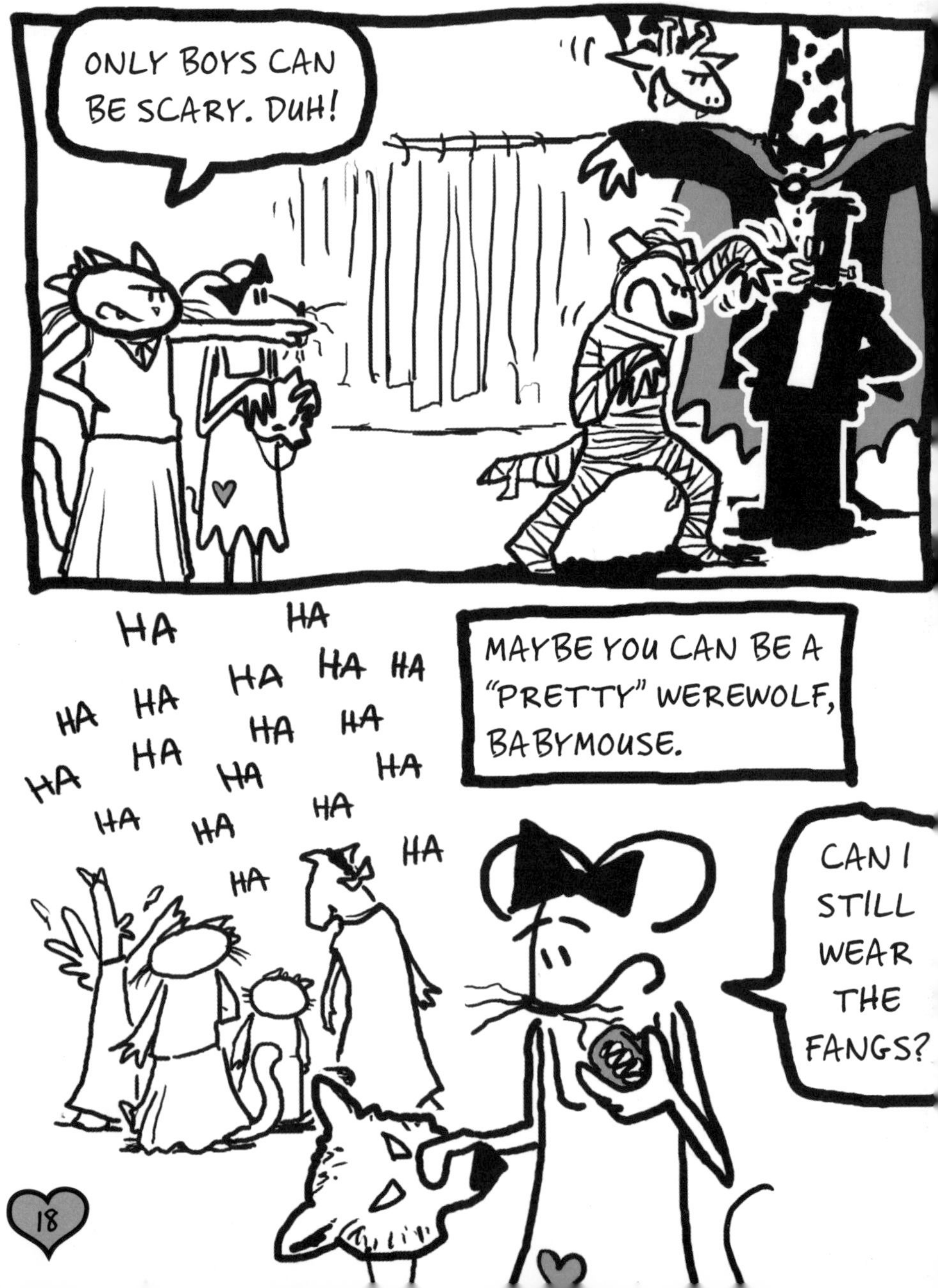
ONLY BOYS CAN BE SCARY. DUH!
HA HA HA HA HA HA HA HA HA HA HA HA HA HA HA HA HA HA HA
MAYBE YOU CAN BE A "PRETTY" WEREWOLF, BABYMOUSE.
CAN I STILL WEAR THE FANGS?

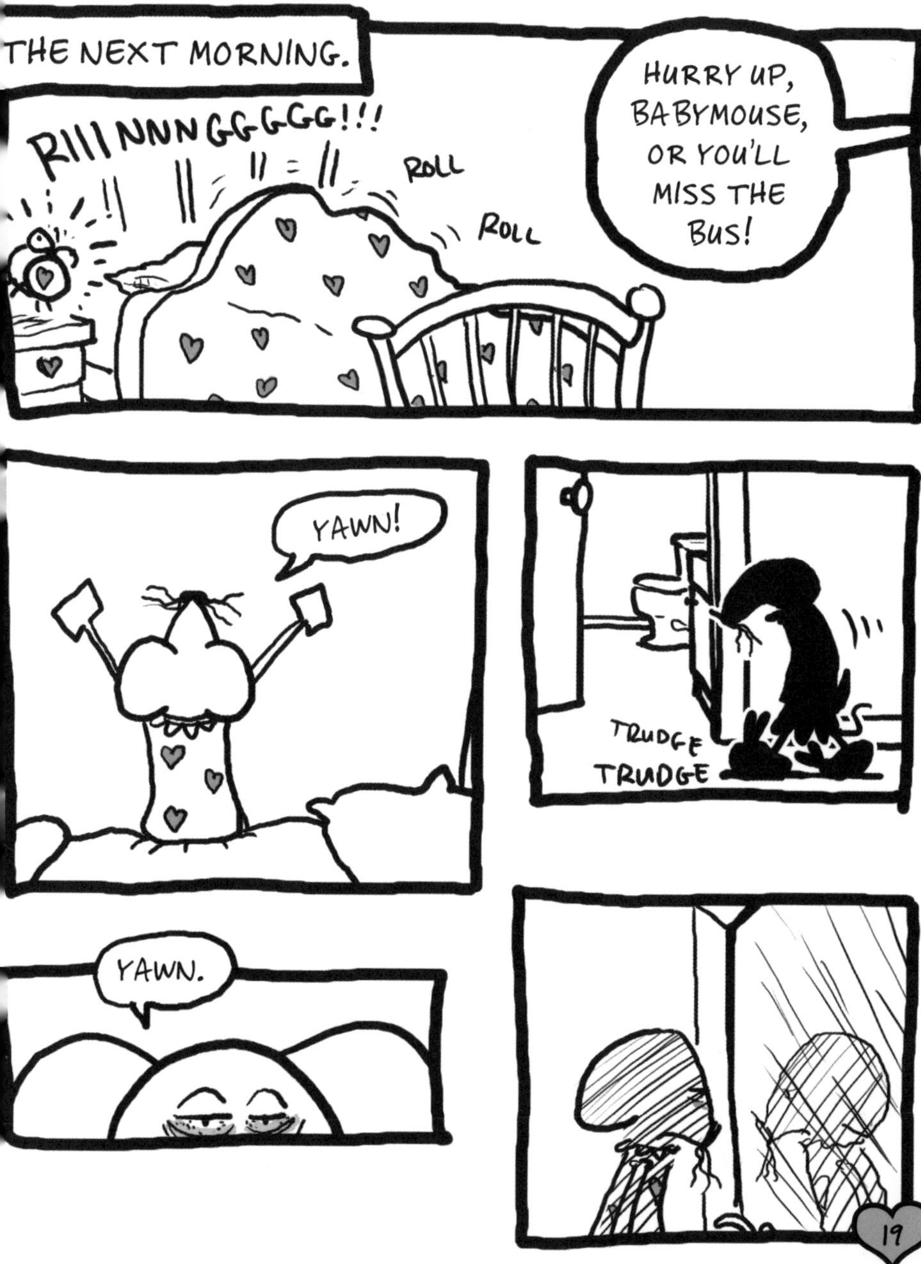
THE NEXT MORNING.
RIIIINNNGGGGG!!!
ROLL
ROLL
HURRY UP, BABYMOUSE, OR YOU'LL MISS THE BUS!
YAWN!
TRUDGE
TRUDGE
YAWN.

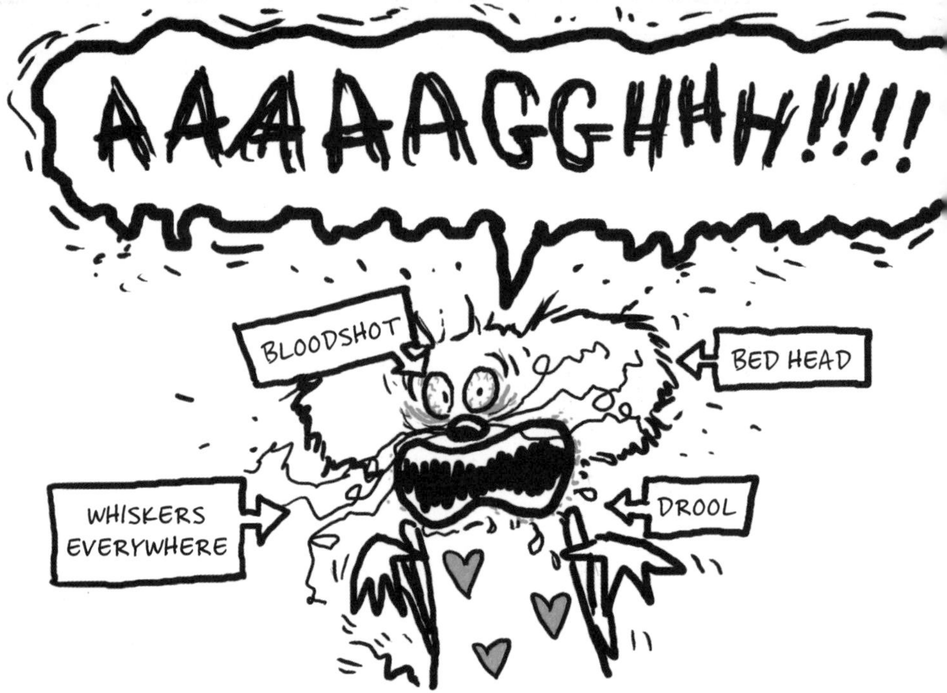
AAAAAAGGHHHH!!!!!
BLOODSHOT
BED HEAD
WHISKERS EVERYWHERE
DROOL

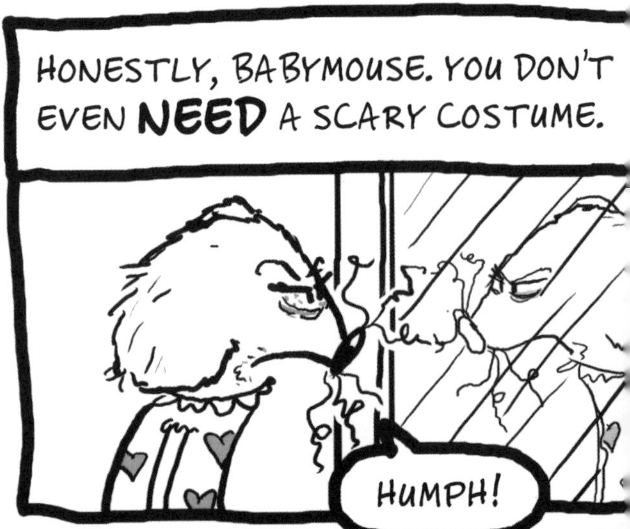
HONESTLY, BABYMOUSE. YOU DON'T EVEN **NEED** A SCARY COSTUME.
HUMPH!

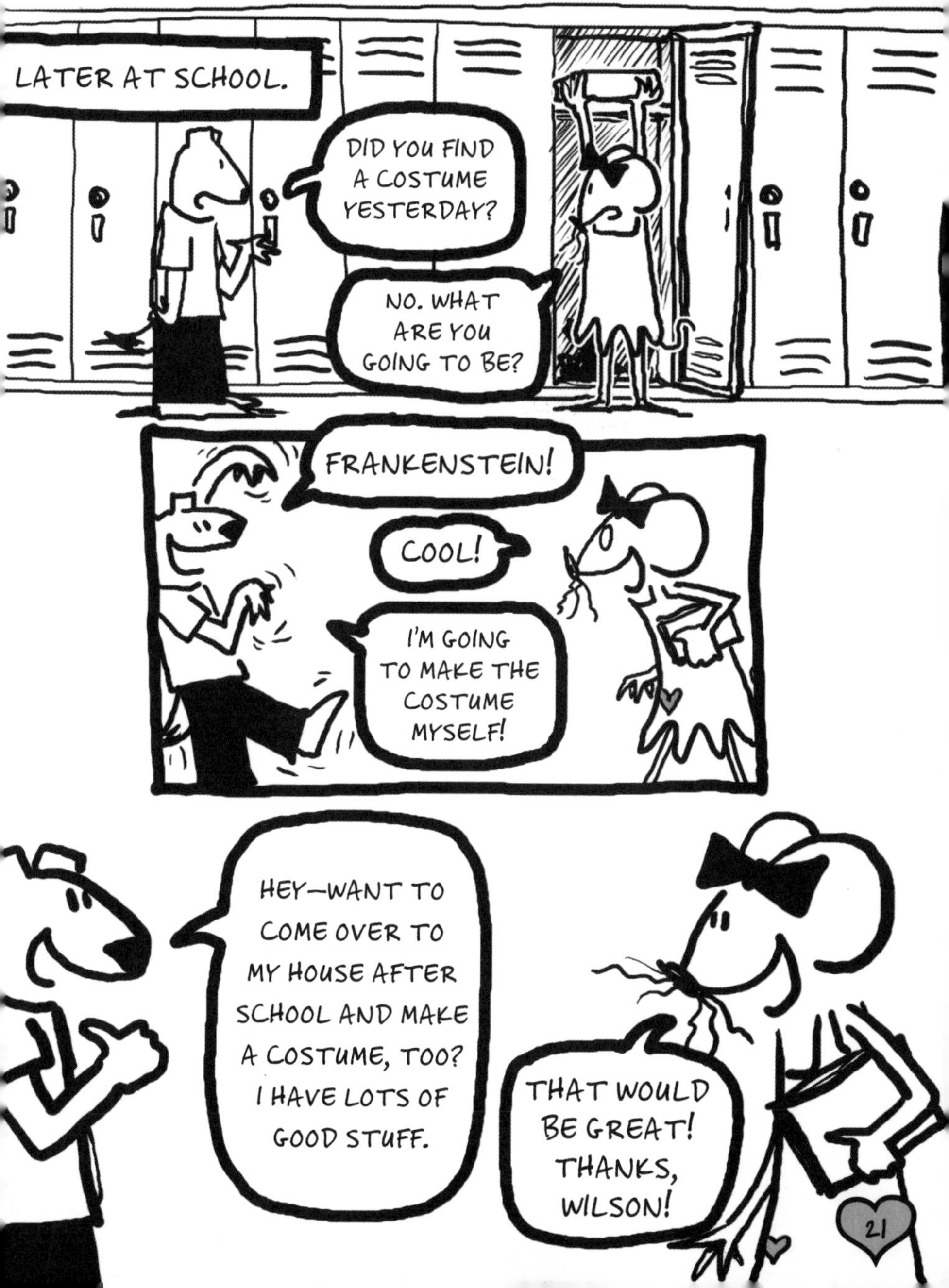
LATER AT SCHOOL.
DID YOU FIND A COSTUME YESTERDAY?
NO. WHAT ARE YOU GOING TO BE?
FRANKENSTEIN!
COOL!
I'M GOING TO MAKE THE COSTUME MYSELF!
HEY—WANT TO COME OVER TO MY HOUSE AFTER SCHOOL AND MAKE A COSTUME, TOO? I HAVE LOTS OF GOOD STUFF.
THAT WOULD BE GREAT! THANKS, WILSON!

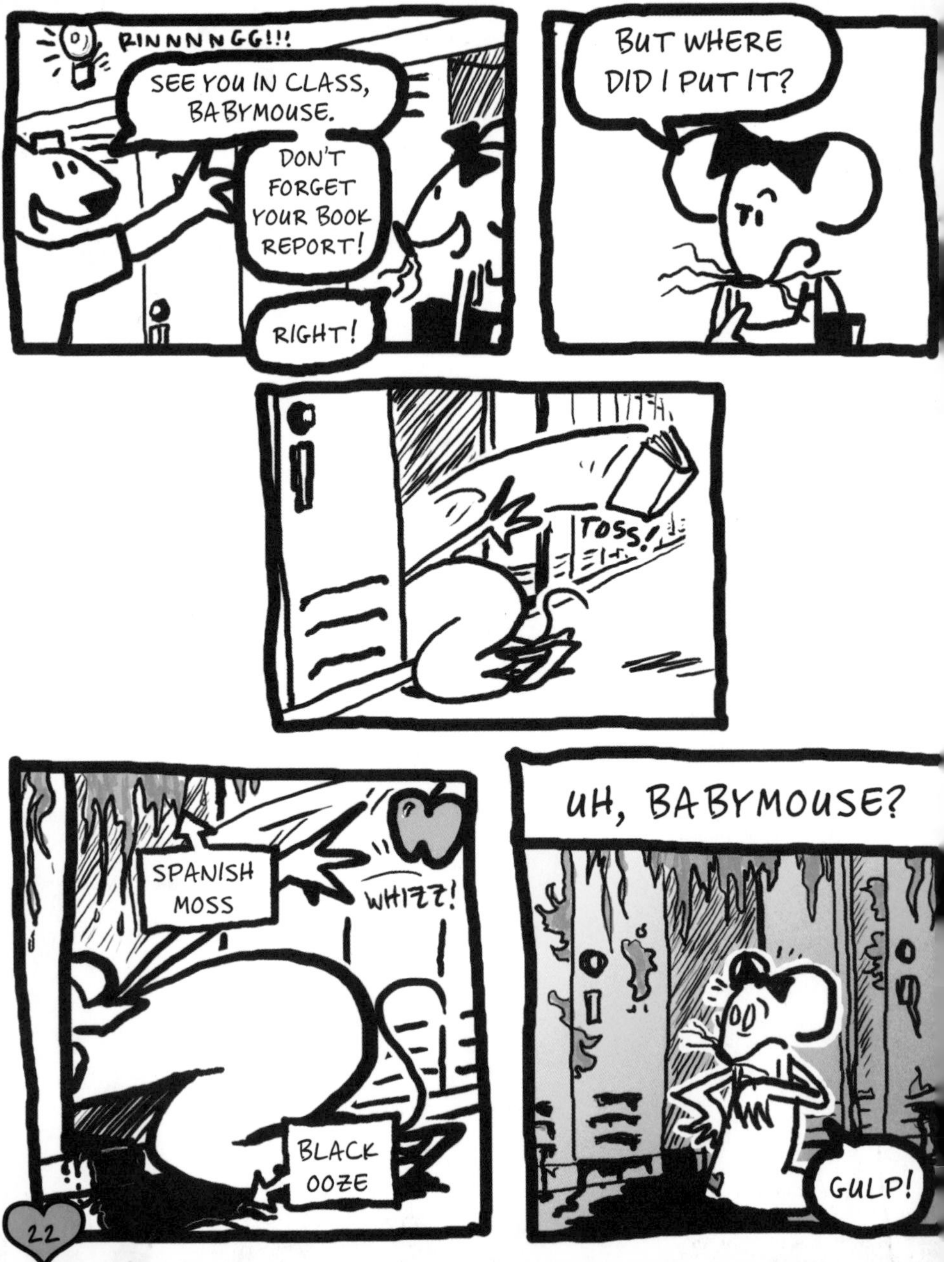
RINNNNGG!!!
SEE YOU IN CLASS, BABYMOUSE.
DON'T FORGET YOUR BOOK REPORT!
RIGHT!
BUT WHERE DID I PUT IT?
TOSS!
SPANISH MOSS
WHIZZ!
BLACK OOZE
UH, BABYMOUSE?
GULP!

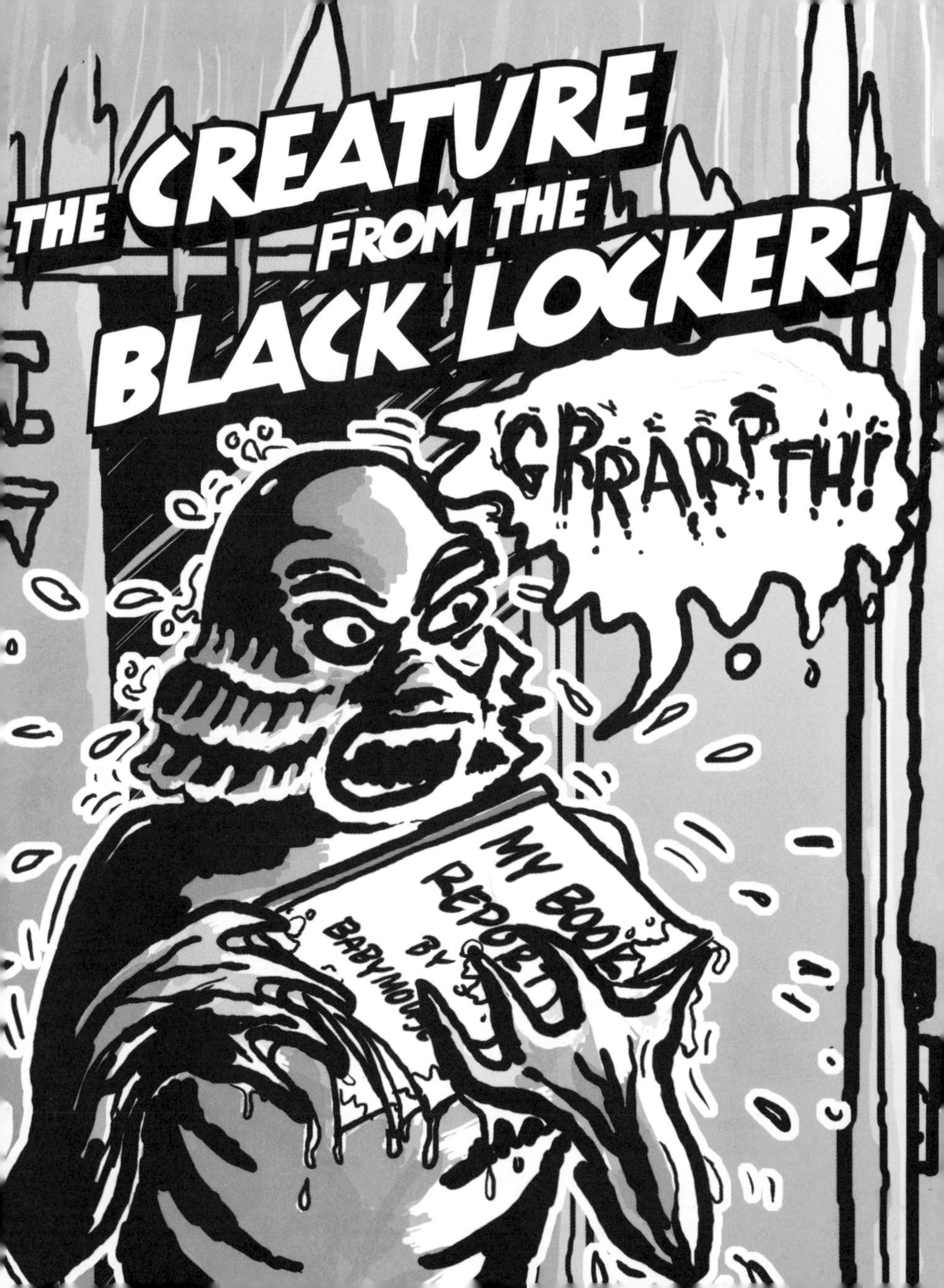
THE CREATURE FROM THE BLACK LOCKER!
GRRRARPTH!
MY BOOK REPORT
BY
BABYMOU

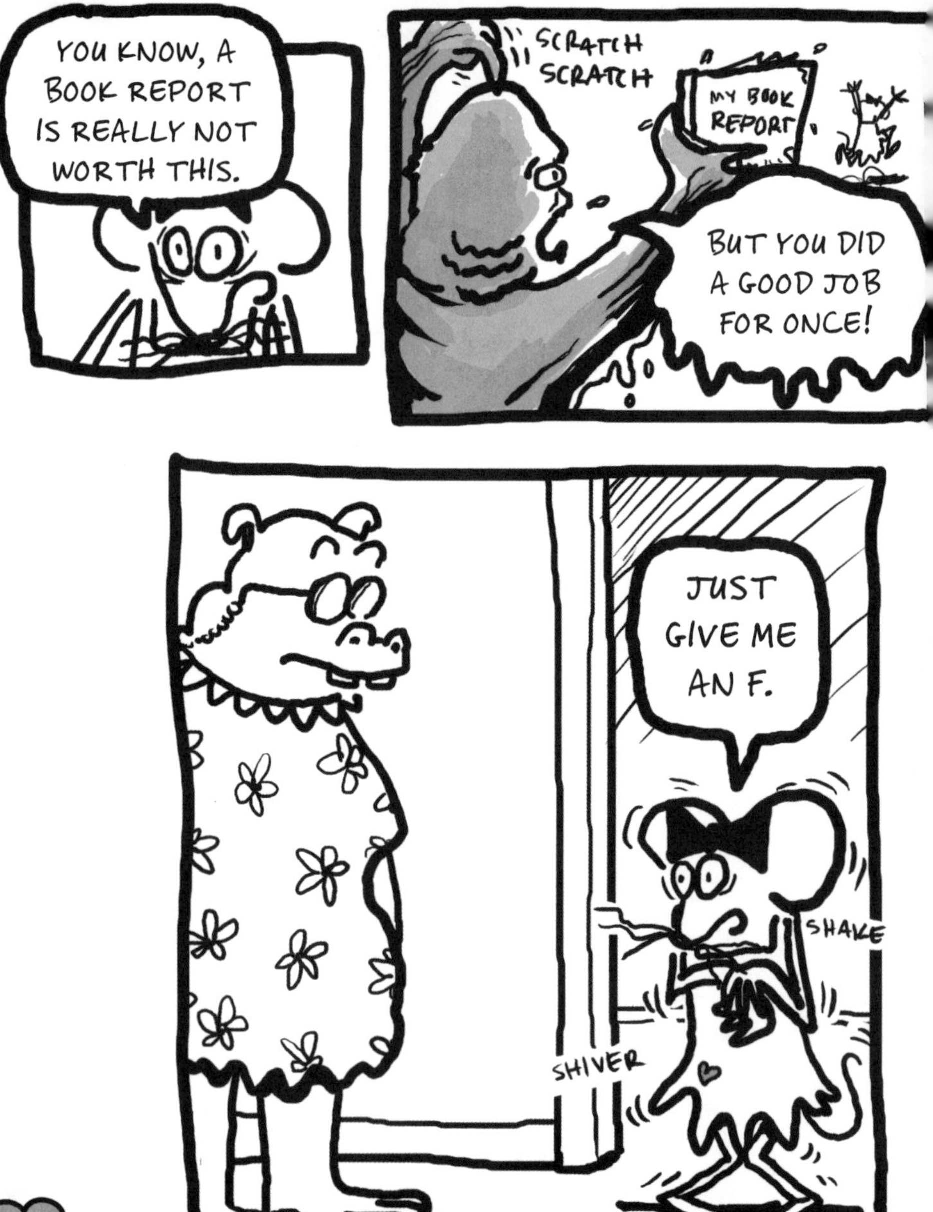
YOU KNOW, A BOOK REPORT IS REALLY NOT WORTH THIS.
SCRATCH SCRATCH
MY BOOK REPORT
BUT YOU DID A GOOD JOB FOR ONCE!
JUST GIVE ME AN F.
SHAKE
SHIVER

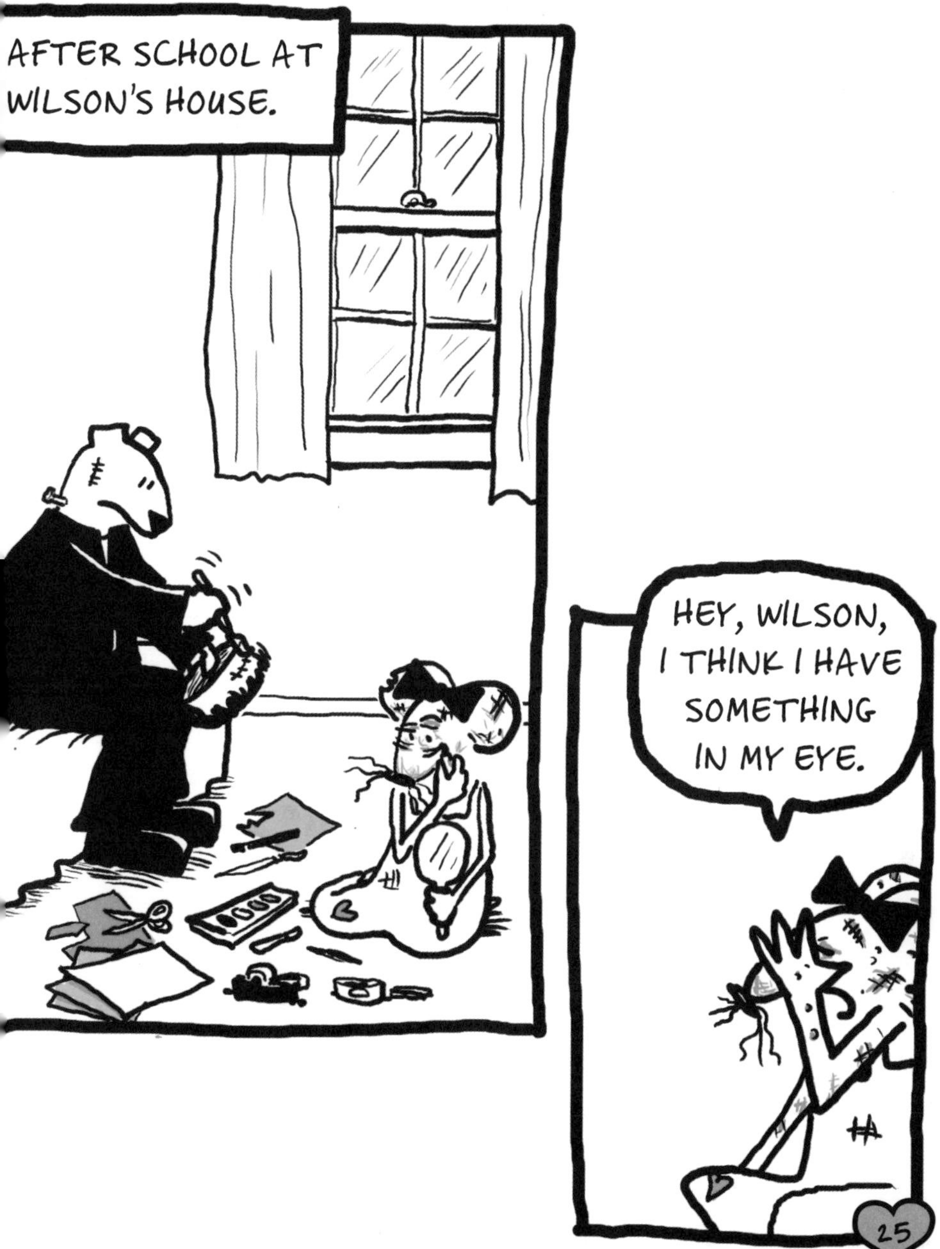

AFTER SCHOOL AT WILSON'S HOUSE.
HEY, WILSON, I THINK I HAVE SOMETHING IN MY EYE.

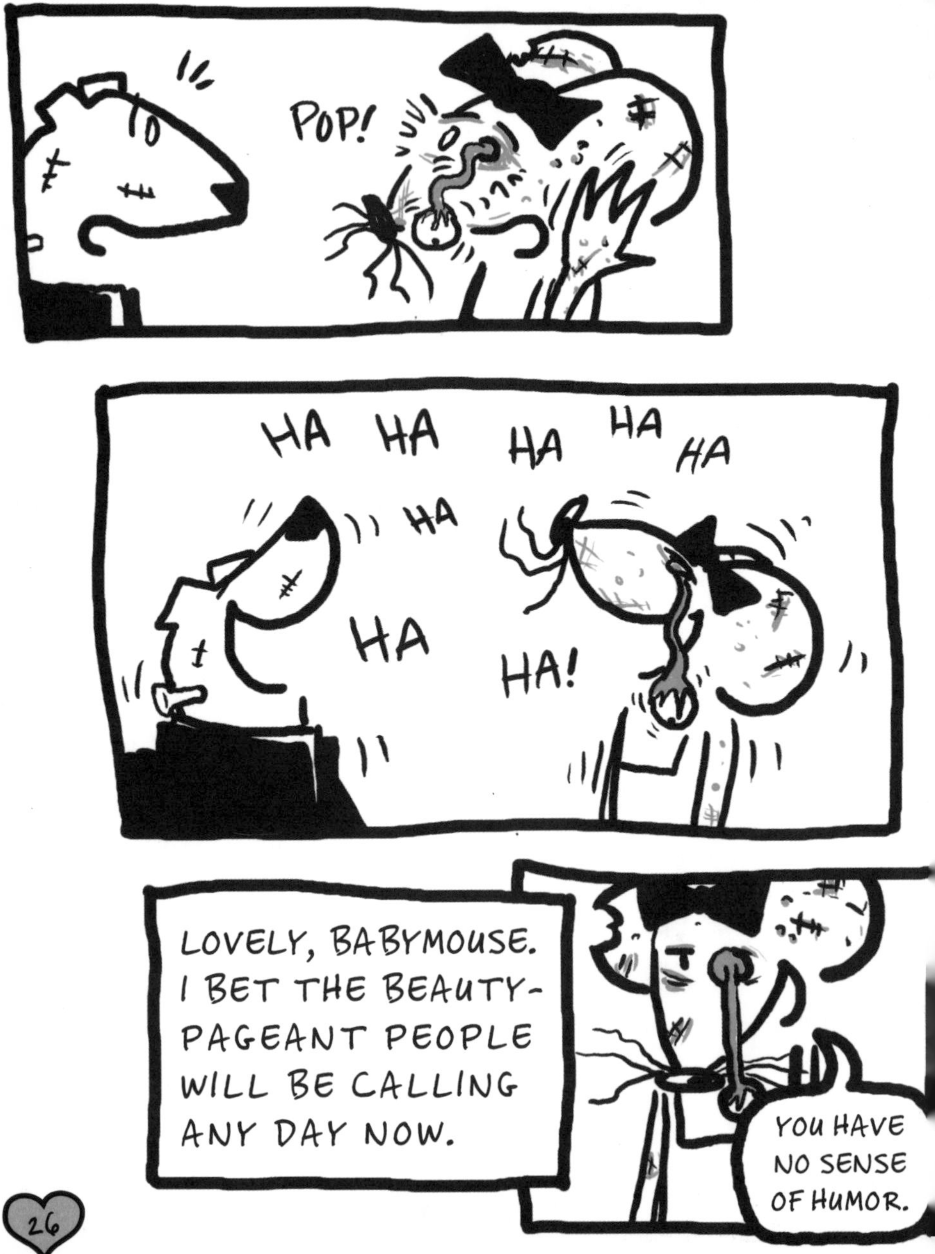
POP!
HA HA HA HA HA
HA
HA
HA!
LOVELY, BABYMOUSE. I BET THE BEAUTY-PAGEANT PEOPLE WILL BE CALLING ANY DAY NOW.
YOU HAVE NO SENSE OF HUMOR.

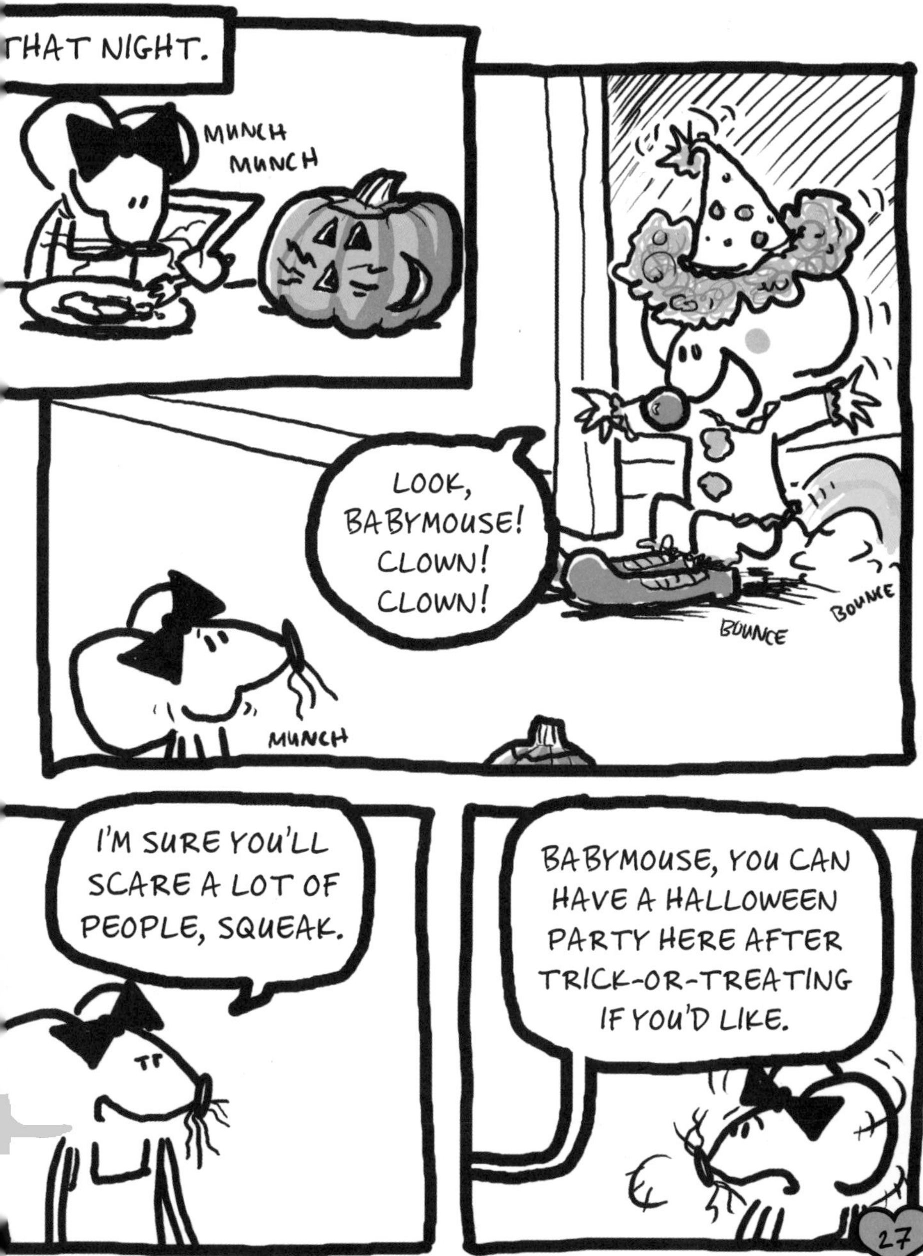

THAT NIGHT.
MUNCH
MUNCH
LOOK, BABYMOUSE! CLOWN! CLOWN!
BOUNCE
BOUNCE
MUNCH
I'M SURE YOU'LL SCARE A LOT OF PEOPLE, SQUEAK.
BABYMOUSE, YOU CAN HAVE A HALLOWEEN PARTY HERE AFTER TRICK-OR-TREATING IF YOU'D LIKE.

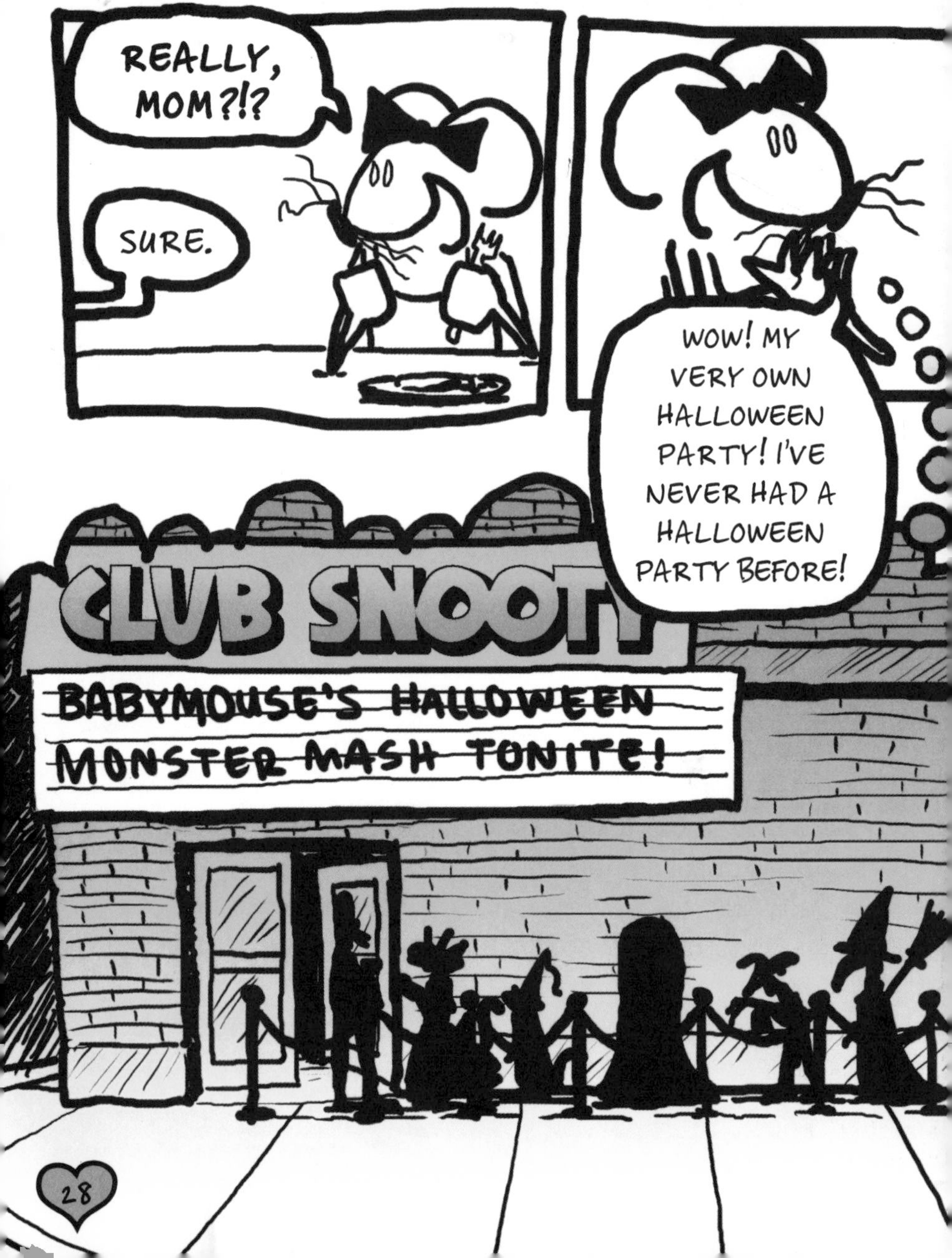
REALLY, MOM?!?
SURE.
WOW! MY VERY OWN HALLOWEEN PARTY! I'VE NEVER HAD A HALLOWEEN PARTY BEFORE!
CLUB SNOOTY
BABYMOUSE'S HALLOWEEN MONSTER MASH TONITE!

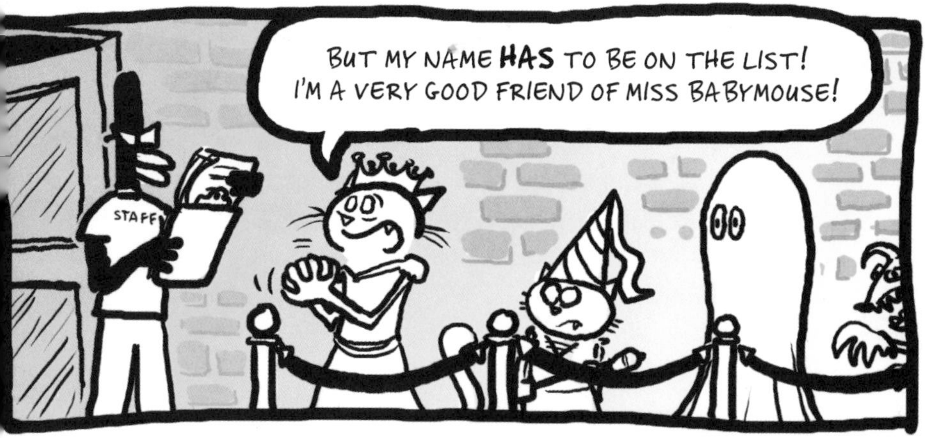
BUT MY NAME **HAS** TO BE ON THE LIST! I'M A VERY GOOD FRIEND OF MISS BABYMOUSE!
STAFF

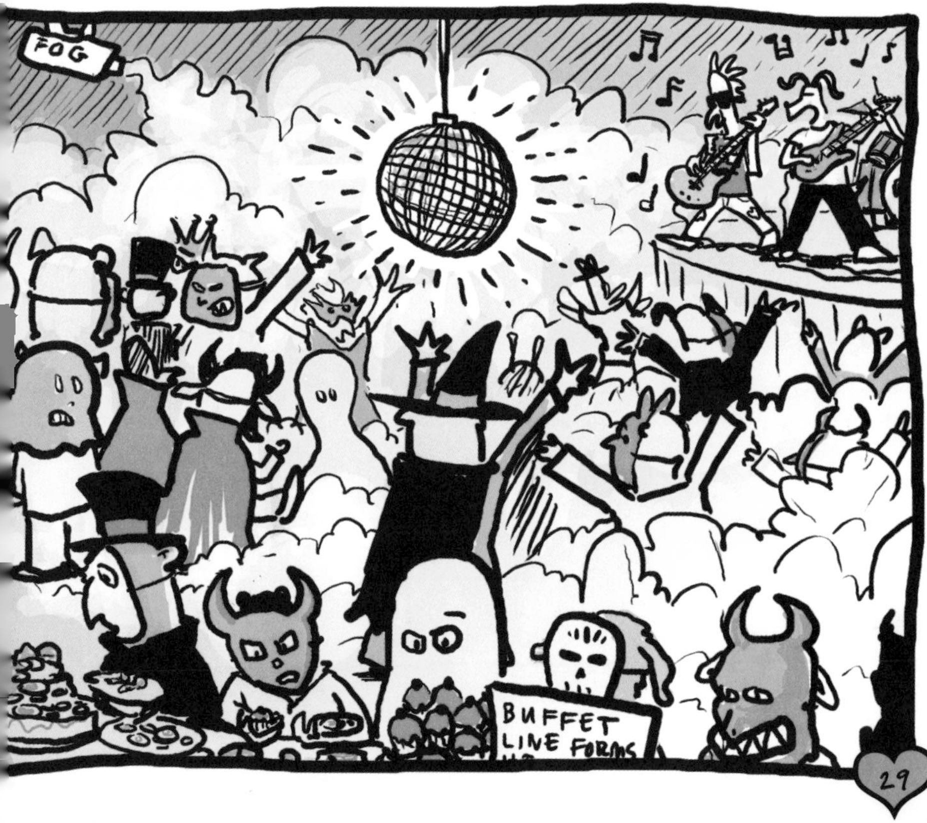
FOG
BUFFET LINE FORMS

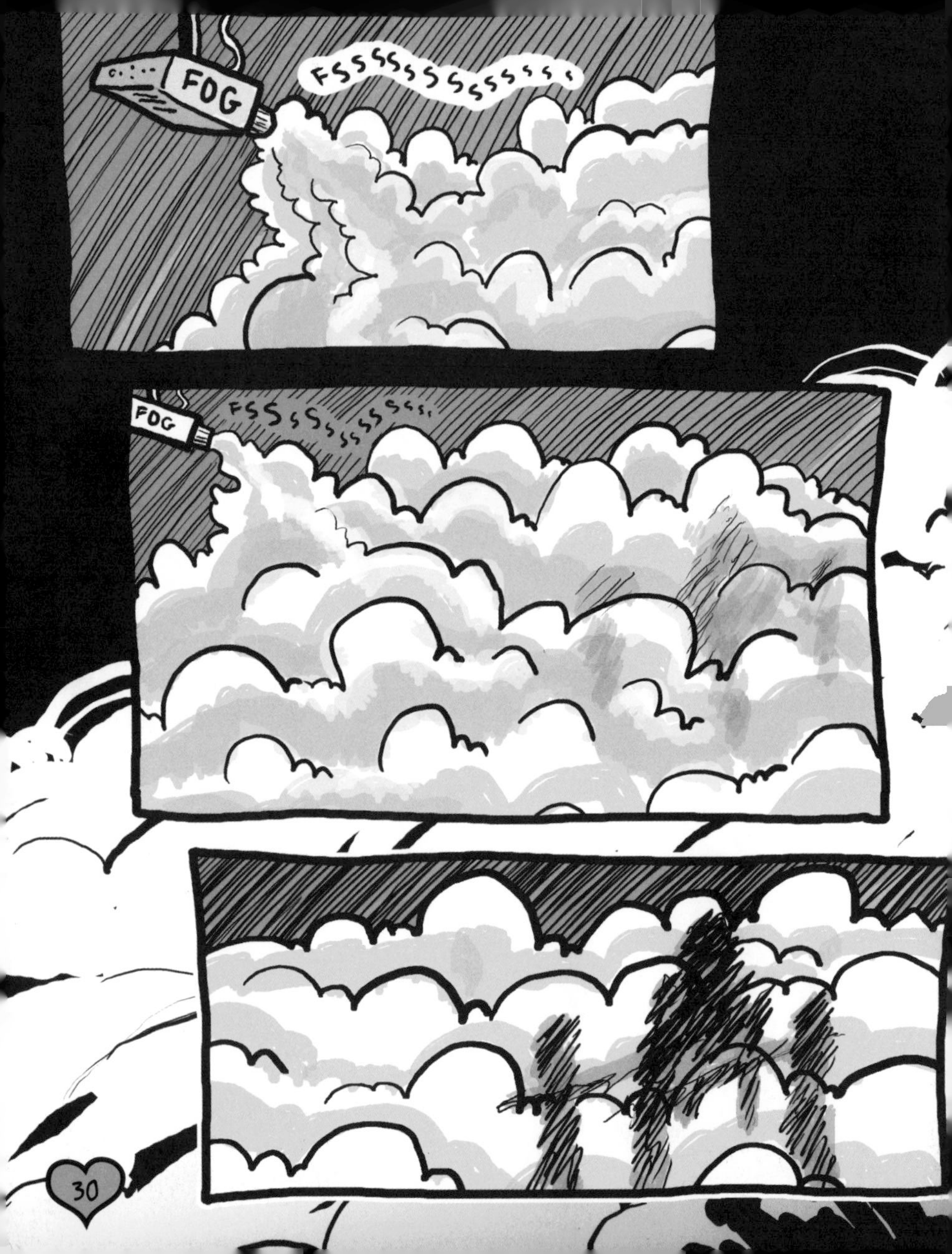
FOG
FSSSSSSSSSSSSSSS
FOG
FSSSSSSSSSSSS

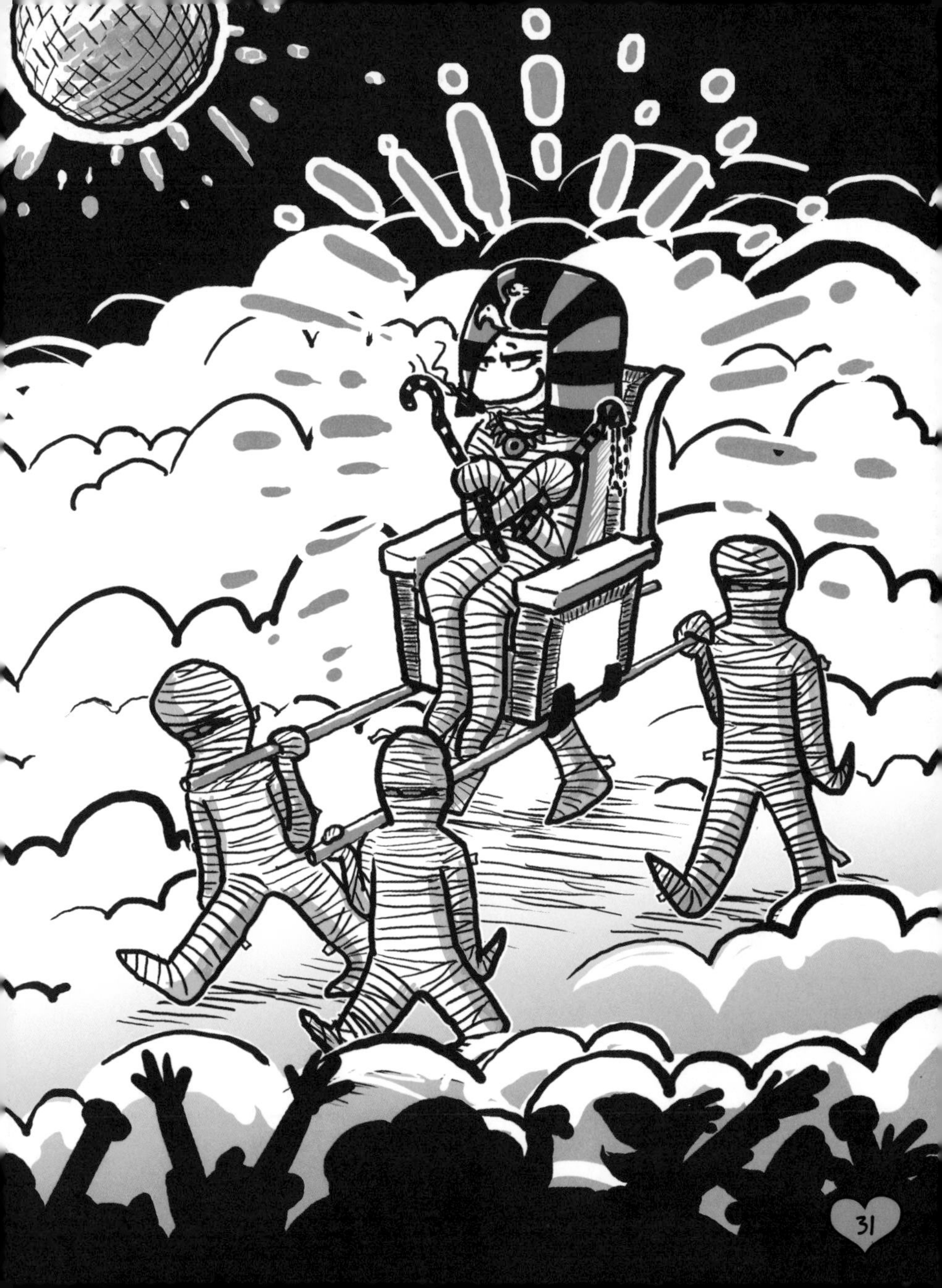

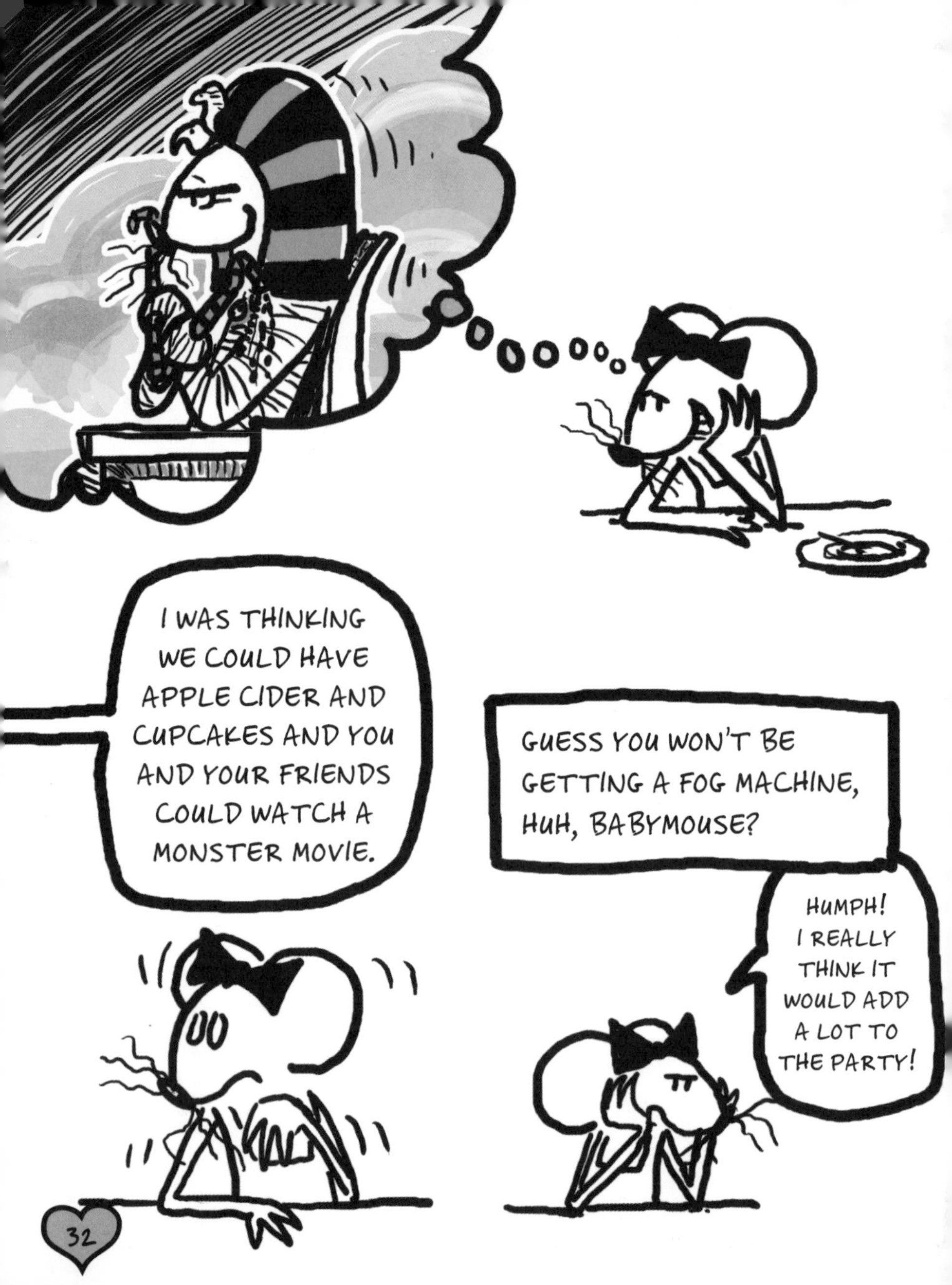

I WAS THINKING WE COULD HAVE APPLE CIDER AND CUPCAKES AND YOU AND YOUR FRIENDS COULD WATCH A MONSTER MOVIE.
GUESS YOU WON'T BE GETTING A FOG MACHINE, HUH, BABYMOUSE?
HUMPH! I REALLY THINK IT WOULD ADD A LOT TO THE PARTY!

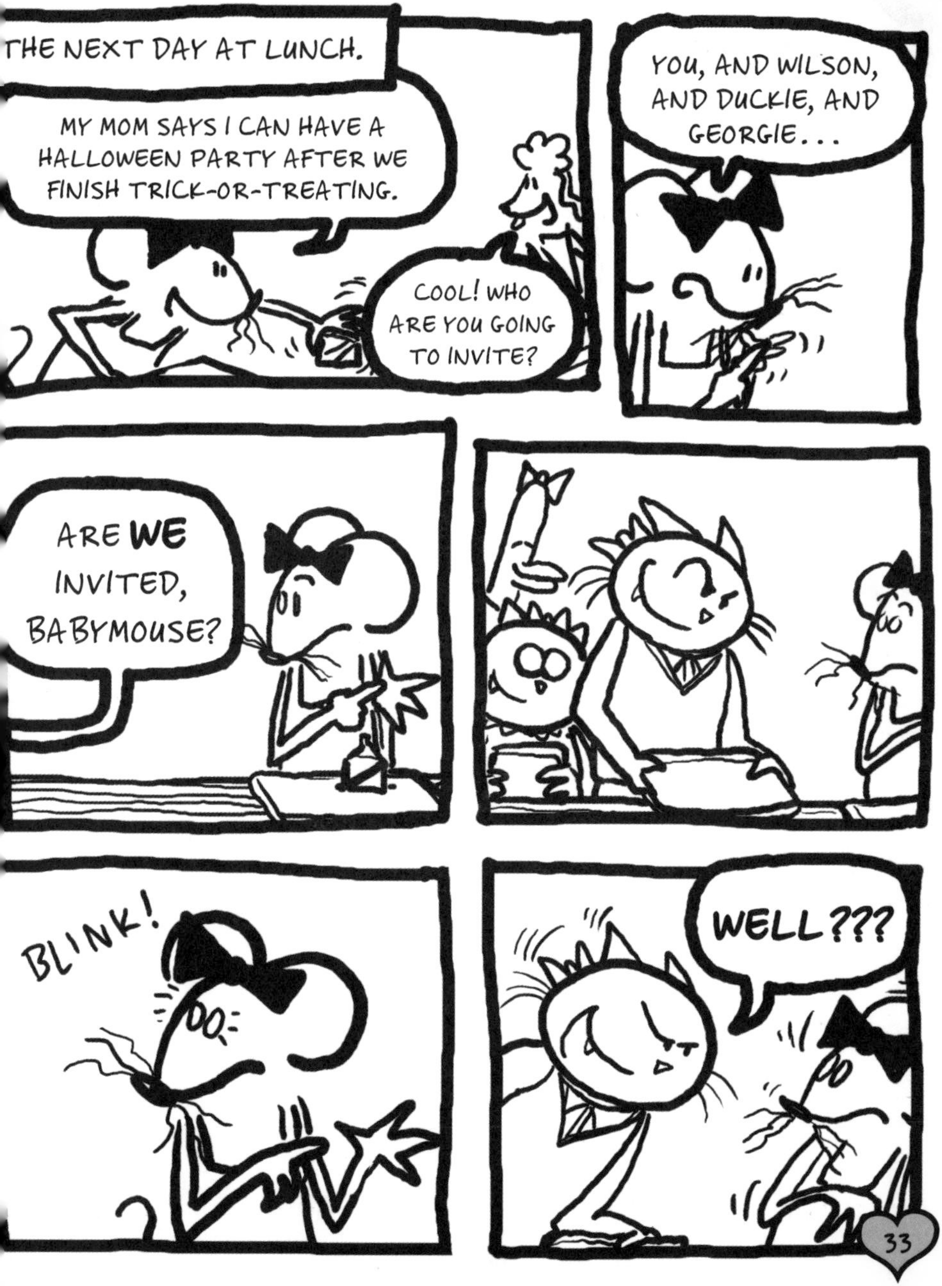
THE NEXT DAY AT LUNCH.
MY MOM SAYS I CAN HAVE A HALLOWEEN PARTY AFTER WE FINISH TRICK-OR-TREATING.
COOL! WHO ARE YOU GOING TO INVITE?
YOU, AND WILSON, AND DUCKIE, AND GEORGIE...
ARE **WE** INVITED, BABYMOUSE?
BLINK!
WELL???

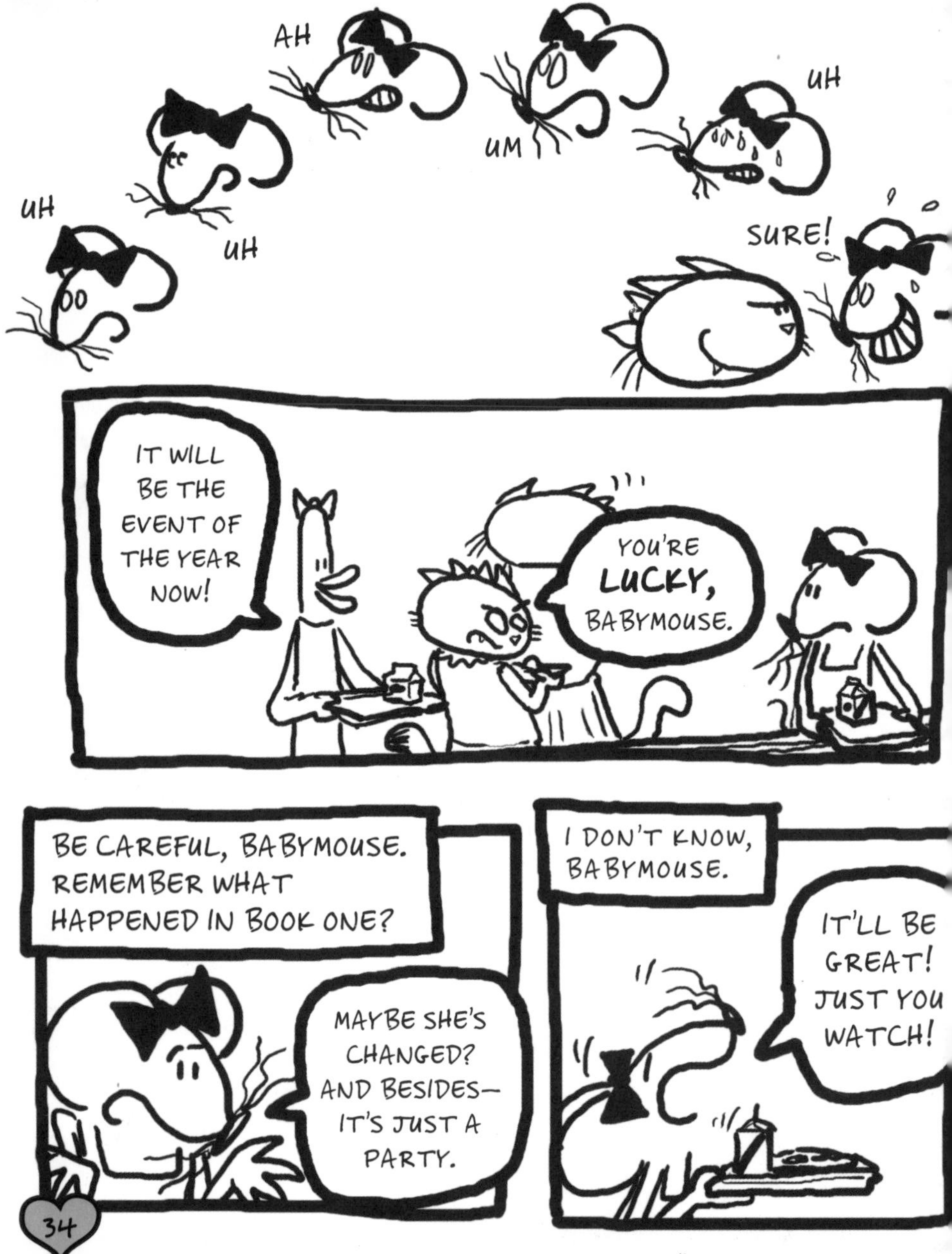
UH
UH
AH
UM
UH
SURE!
IT WILL BE THE EVENT OF THE YEAR NOW!
YOU'RE **LUCKY,** BABYMOUSE.
BE CAREFUL, BABYMOUSE. REMEMBER WHAT HAPPENED IN BOOK ONE?
MAYBE SHE'S CHANGED? AND BESIDES— IT'S JUST A PARTY.
I DON'T KNOW, BABYMOUSE.
IT'LL BE GREAT! JUST YOU WATCH!

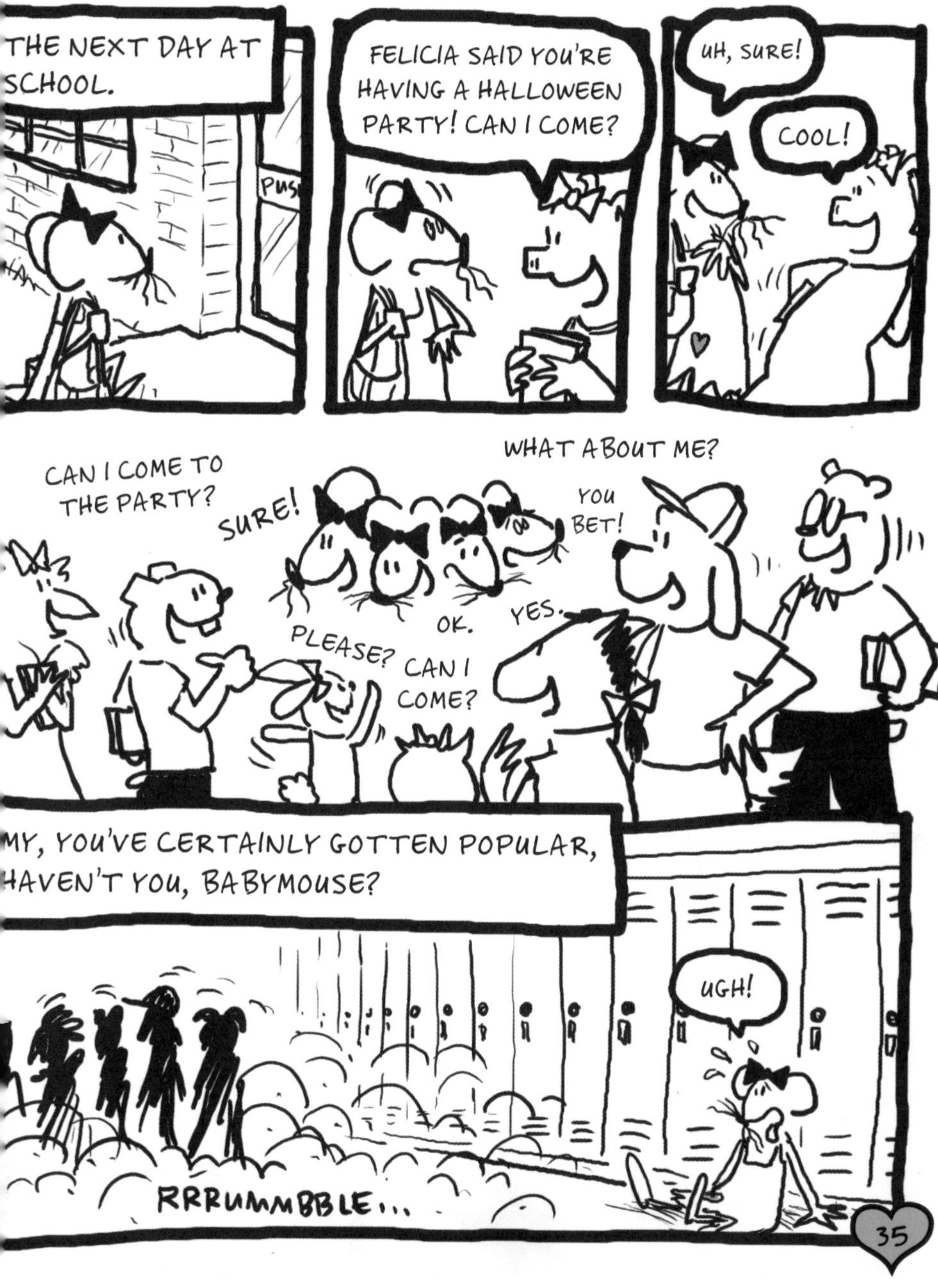
THE NEXT DAY AT SCHOOL.
PUSH
FELICIA SAID YOU'RE HAVING A HALLOWEEN PARTY! CAN I COME?
UH, SURE!
COOL!
CAN I COME TO THE PARTY?
SURE!
WHAT ABOUT ME?
YOU BET!
PLEASE?
OK.
YES.
CAN I COME?
MY, YOU'VE CERTAINLY GOTTEN POPULAR, HAVEN'T YOU, BABYMOUSE?
UGH!
RRRUMMBBLE...

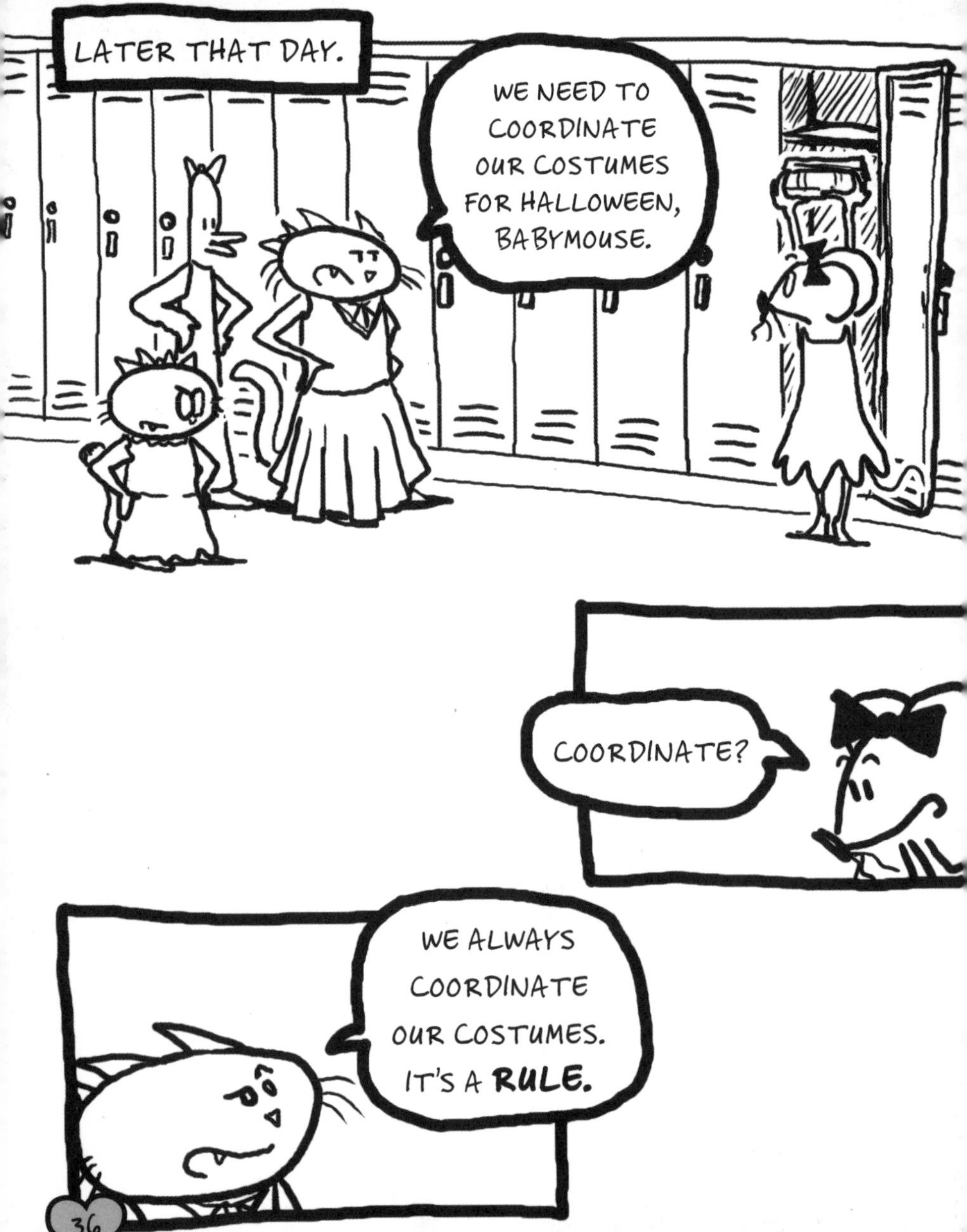
LATER THAT DAY.
WE NEED TO COORDINATE OUR COSTUMES FOR HALLOWEEN, BABYMOUSE.
COORDINATE?
WE ALWAYS COORDINATE OUR COSTUMES. IT'S A **RULE.**

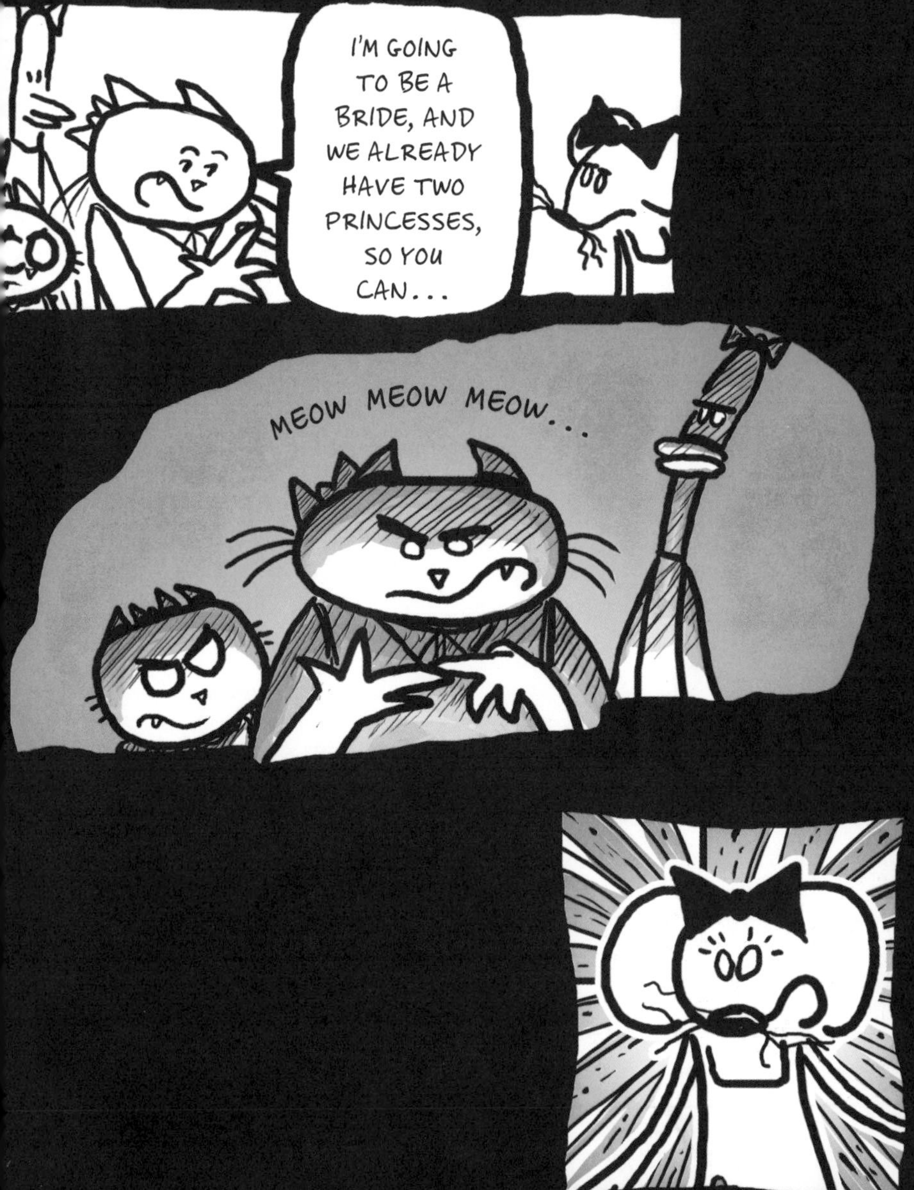
I'M GOING TO BE A BRIDE, AND WE ALREADY HAVE TWO PRINCESSES, SO YOU CAN...
MEOW MEOW MEOW....

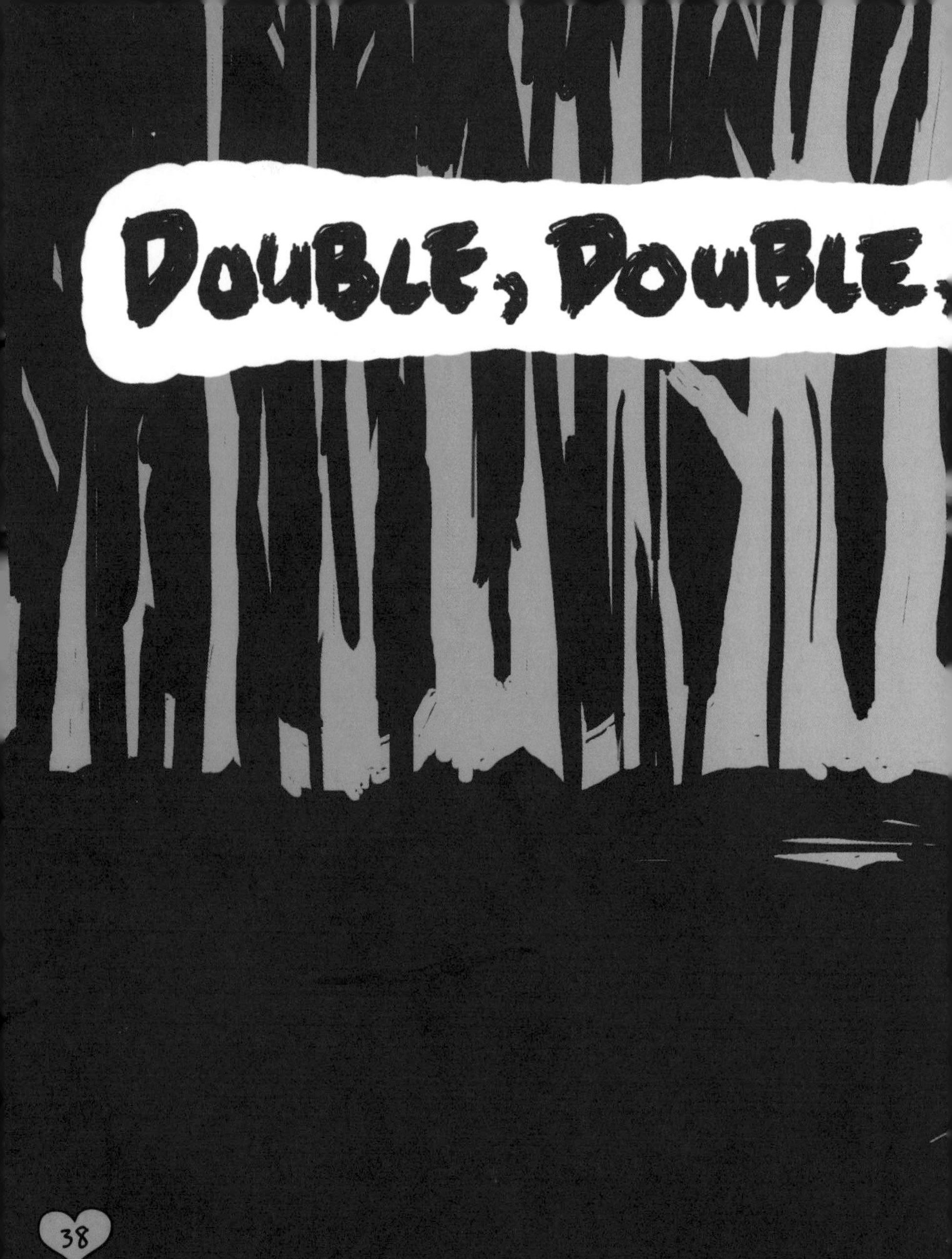
DOUBLE, DOUBLE,

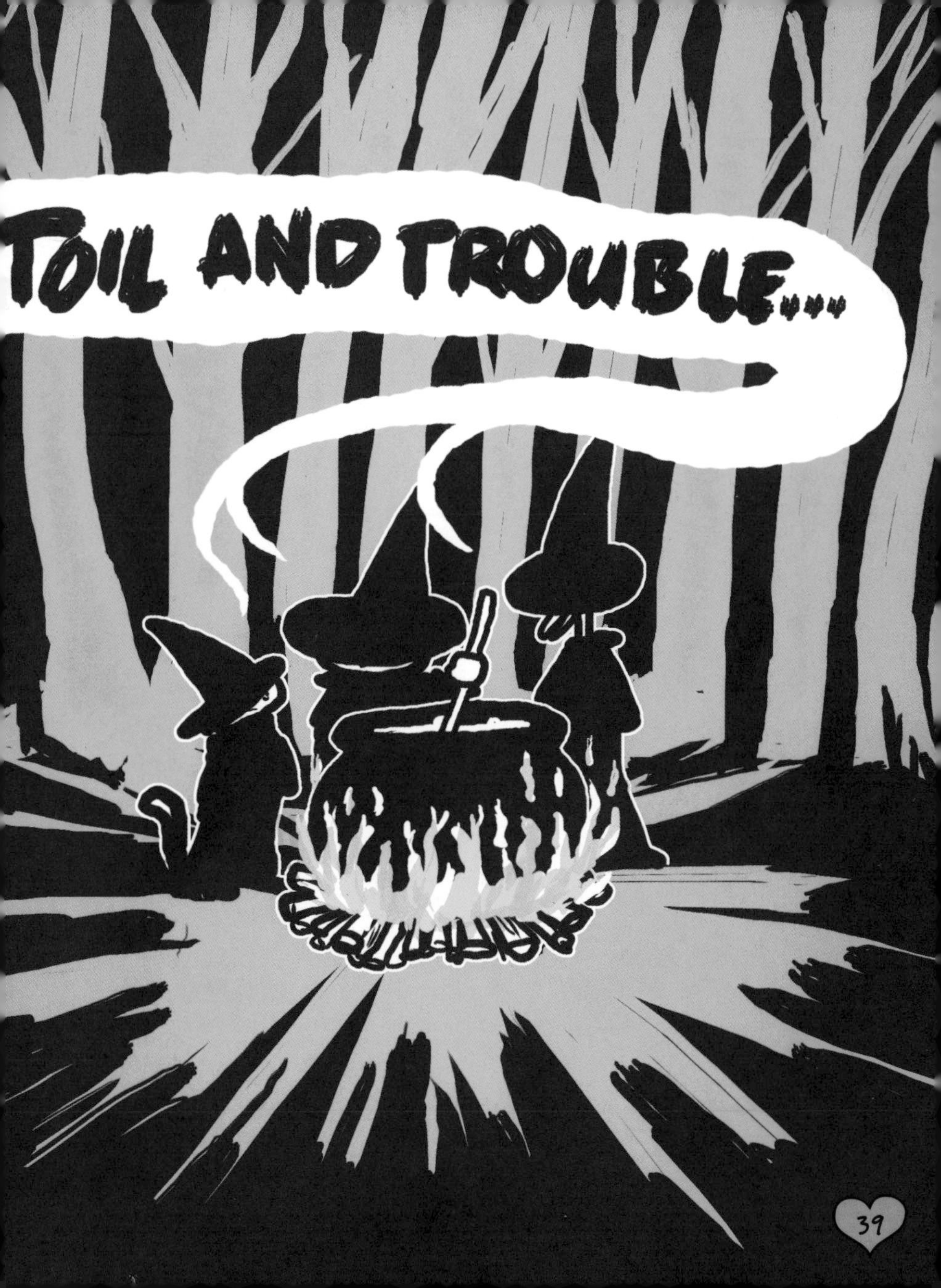
TOIL AND TROUBLE...

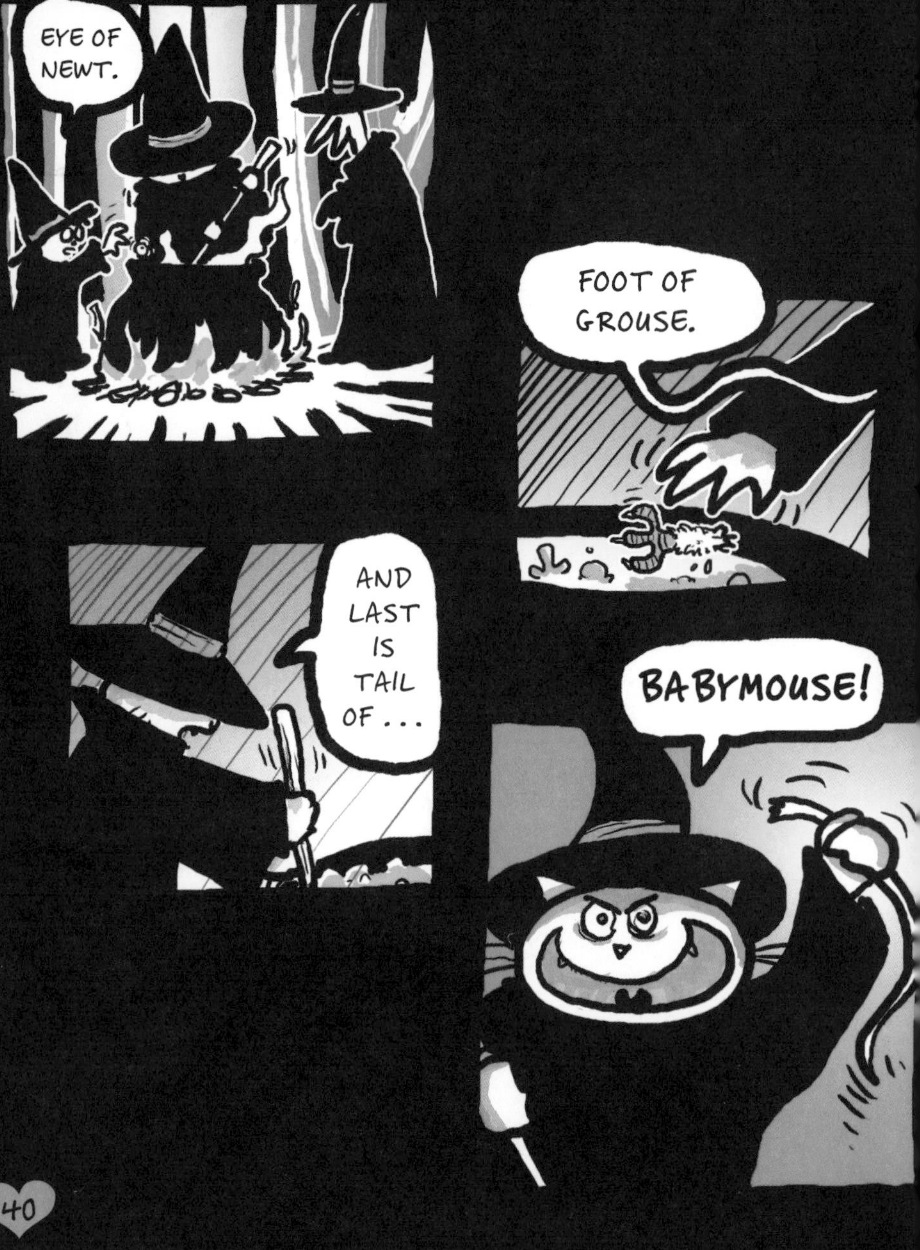
EYE OF NEWT.
FOOT OF GROUSE.
AND LAST IS TAIL OF . . .
BABYMOUSE!

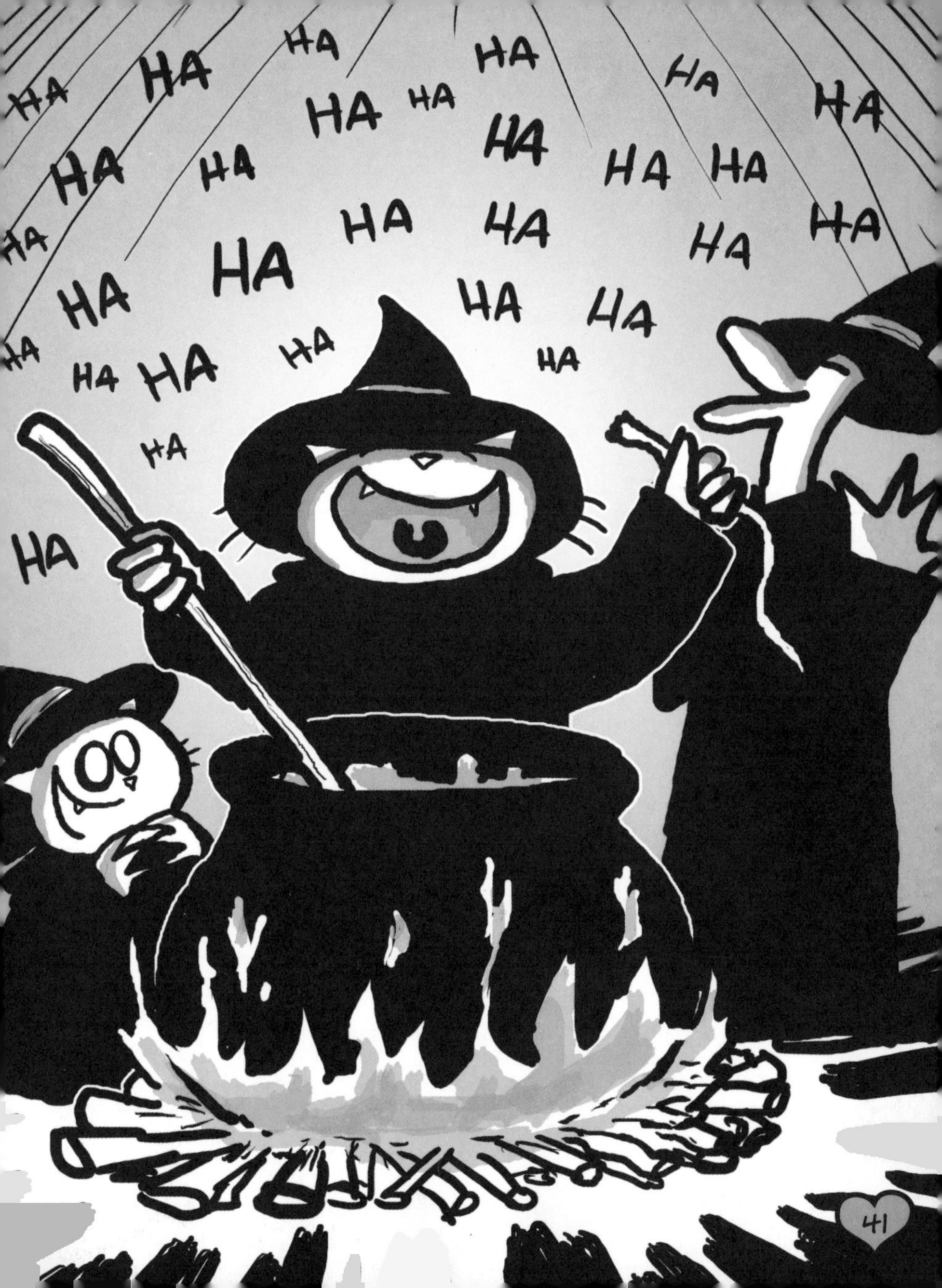
HA HA HA HA HA HA HA HA HA HA HA HA HA HA HA HA HA HA HA HA HA HA HA HA HA HA HA HA HA

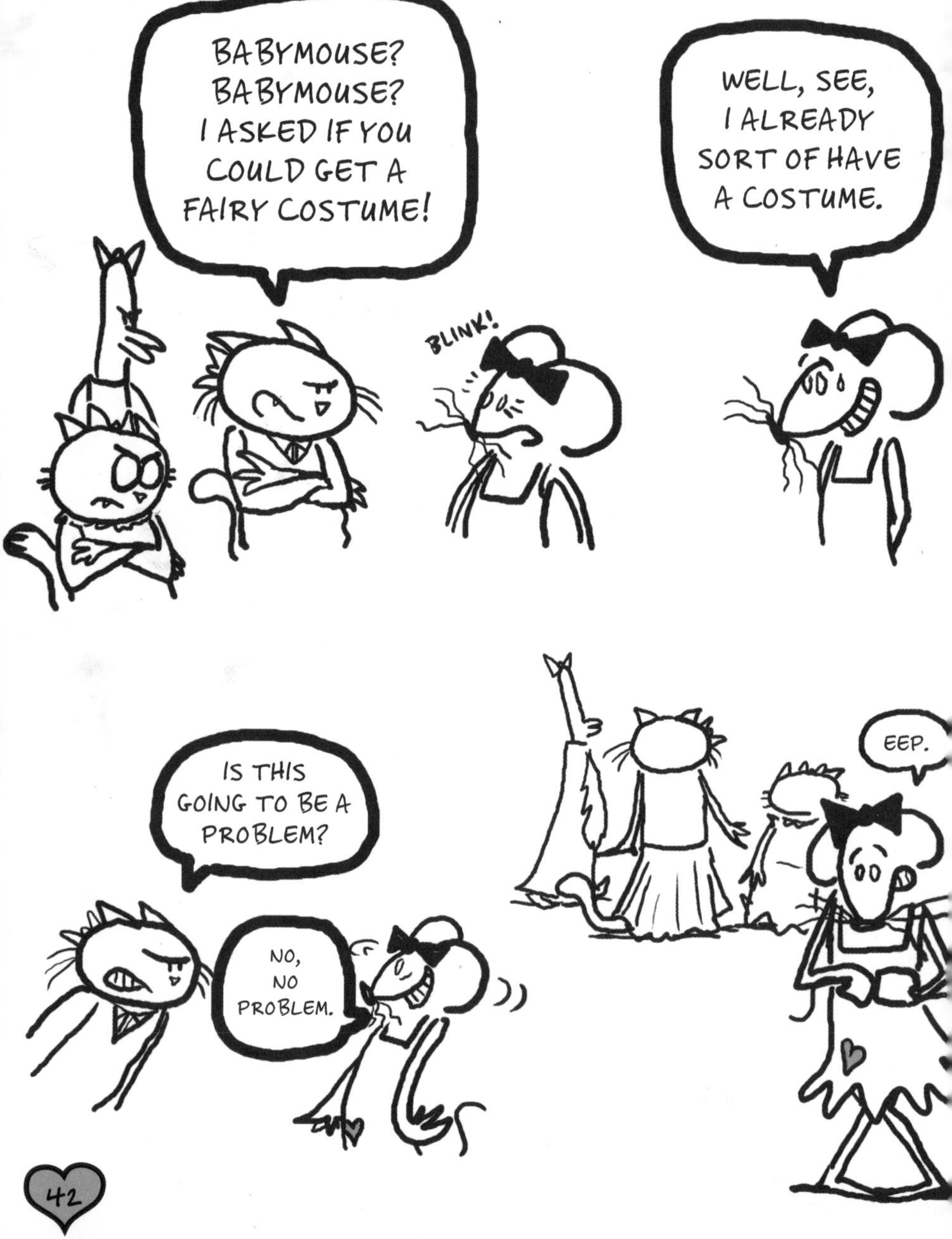
BABYMOUSE? BABYMOUSE? I ASKED IF YOU COULD GET A FAIRY COSTUME!
BLINK!
WELL, SEE, I ALREADY SORT OF HAVE A COSTUME.
IS THIS GOING TO BE A PROBLEM?
NO, NO PROBLEM.
EEP.

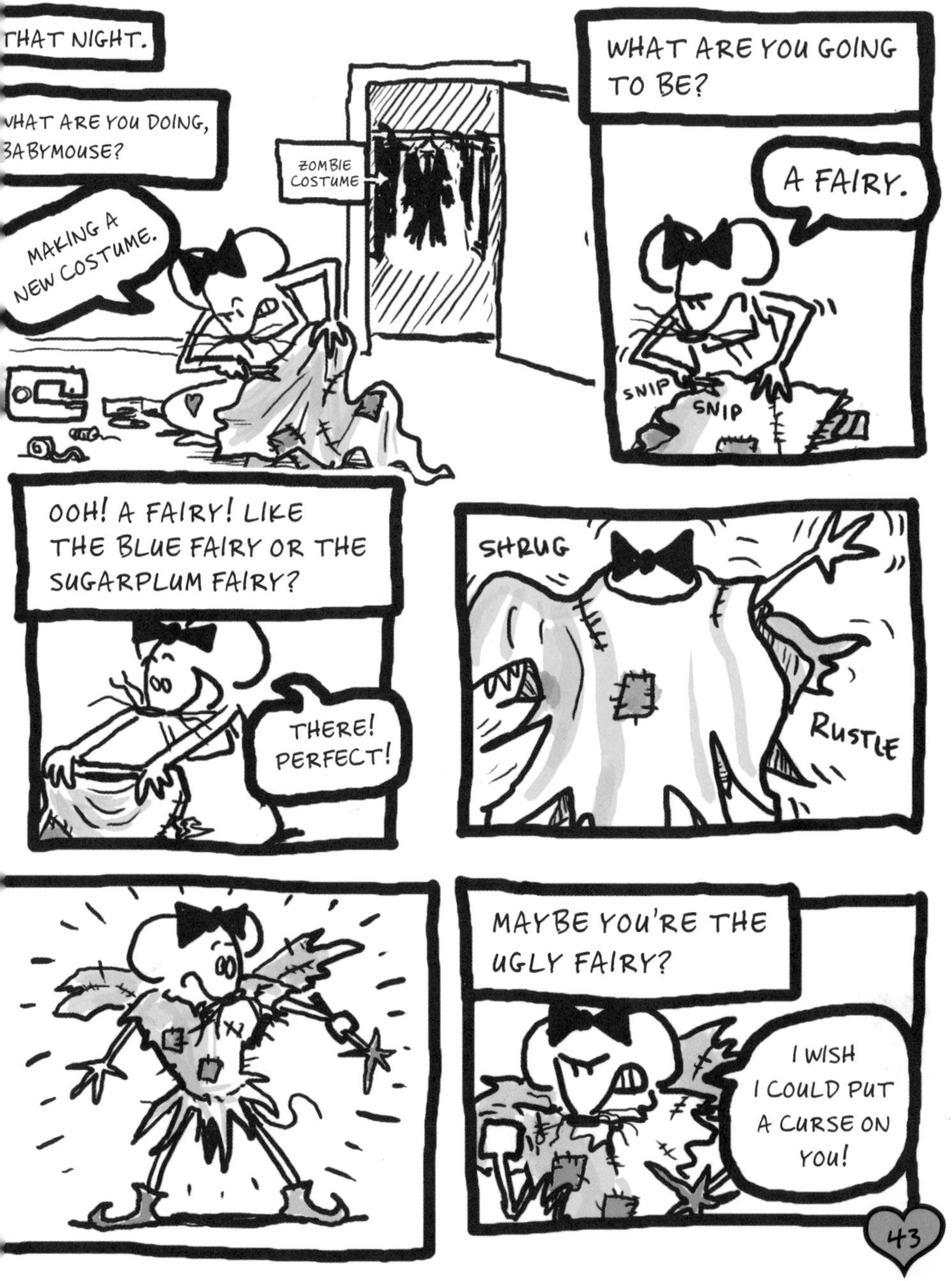
THAT NIGHT.
WHAT ARE YOU DOING, BABYMOUSE?
MAKING A NEW COSTUME.
ZOMBIE COSTUME
WHAT ARE YOU GOING TO BE?
A FAIRY.
SNIP
SNIP
OOH! A FAIRY! LIKE THE BLUE FAIRY OR THE SUGARPLUM FAIRY?
THERE! PERFECT!
SHRUG
RUSTLE
MAYBE YOU'RE THE UGLY FAIRY?
I WISH I COULD PUT A CURSE ON YOU!

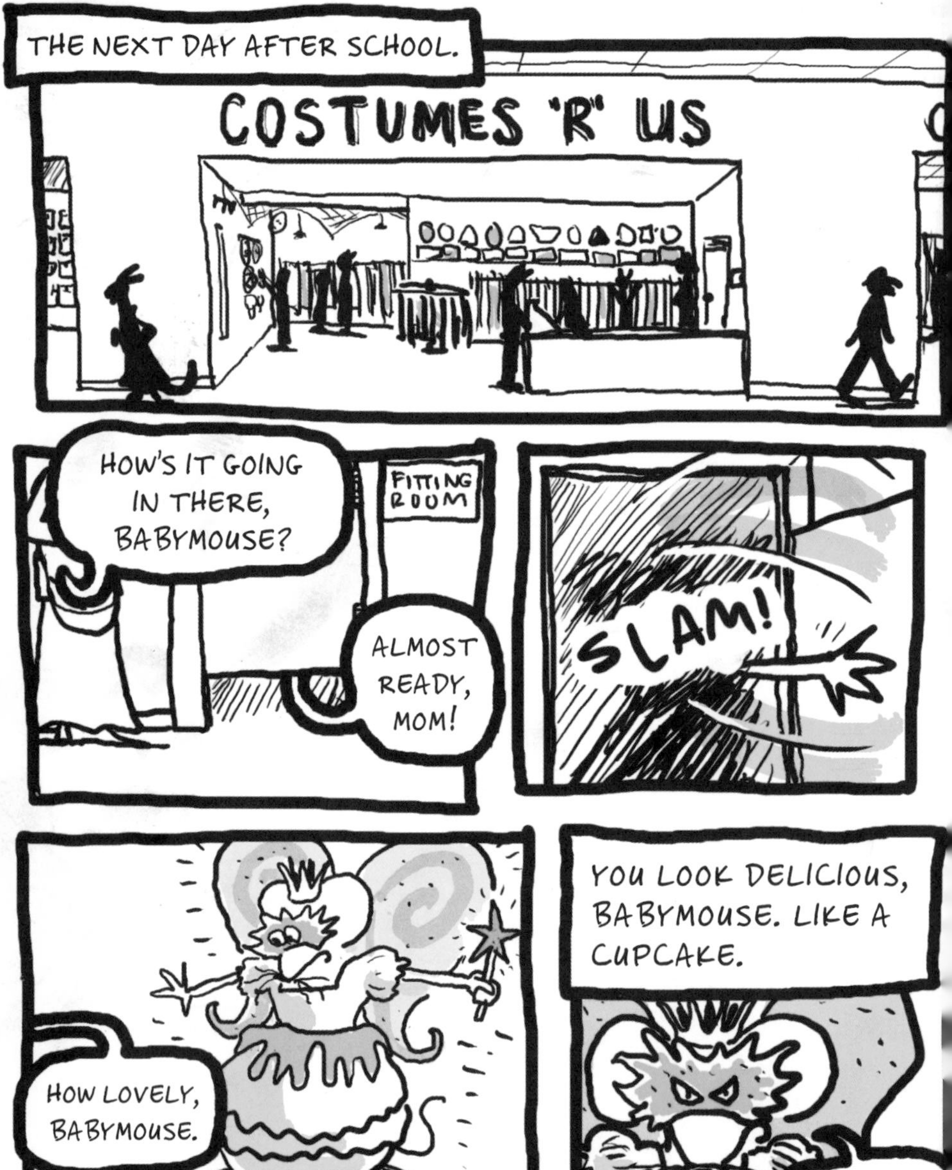
THE NEXT DAY AFTER SCHOOL.
COSTUMES 'R' US
HOW'S IT GOING IN THERE, BABYMOUSE?
FITTING ROOM
ALMOST READY, MOM!
SLAM!
HOW LOVELY, BABYMOUSE.
YOU LOOK DELICIOUS, BABYMOUSE. LIKE A CUPCAKE.
THANKS.

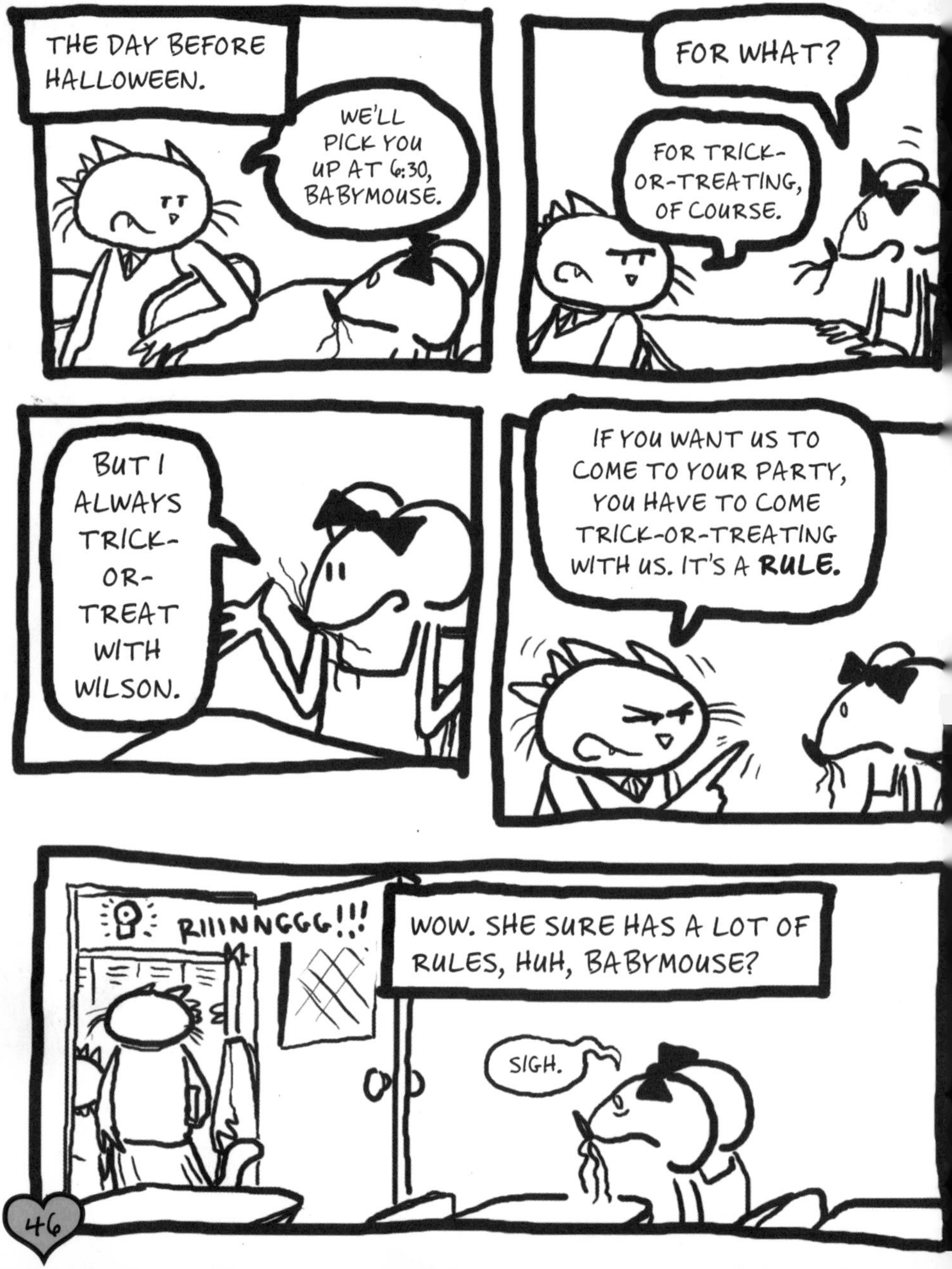
THE DAY BEFORE HALLOWEEN.
WE'LL PICK YOU UP AT 6:30, BABYMOUSE.
FOR WHAT?
FOR TRICK-OR-TREATING, OF COURSE.
BUT I ALWAYS TRICK-OR-TREAT WITH WILSON.
IF YOU WANT US TO COME TO YOUR PARTY, YOU HAVE TO COME TRICK-OR-TREATING WITH US. IT'S A **RULE.**
RIIINNGGG!!!
WOW. SHE SURE HAS A LOT OF RULES, HUH, BABYMOUSE?
SIGH.

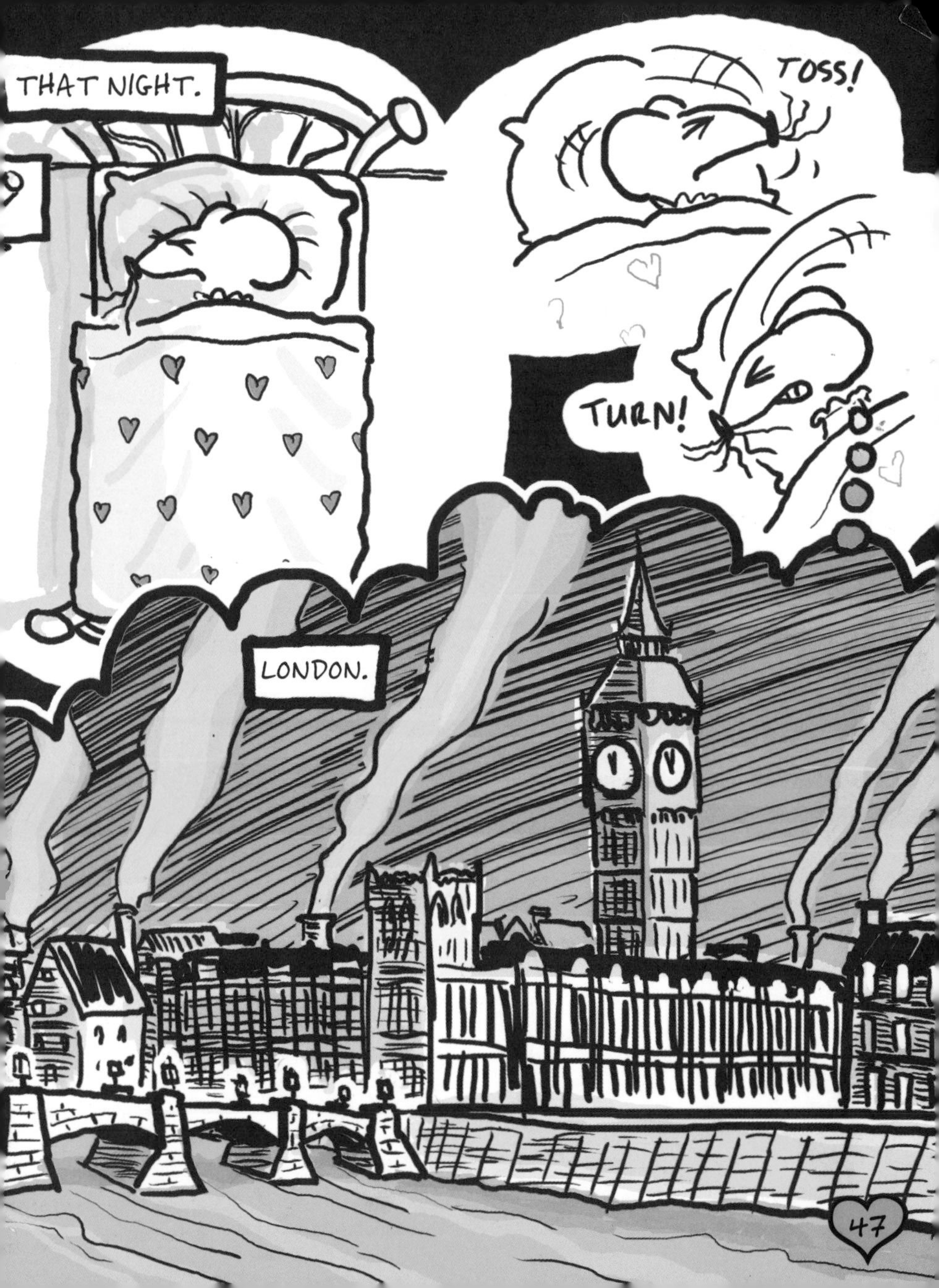
THAT NIGHT.
TOSS!
TURN!
LONDON.

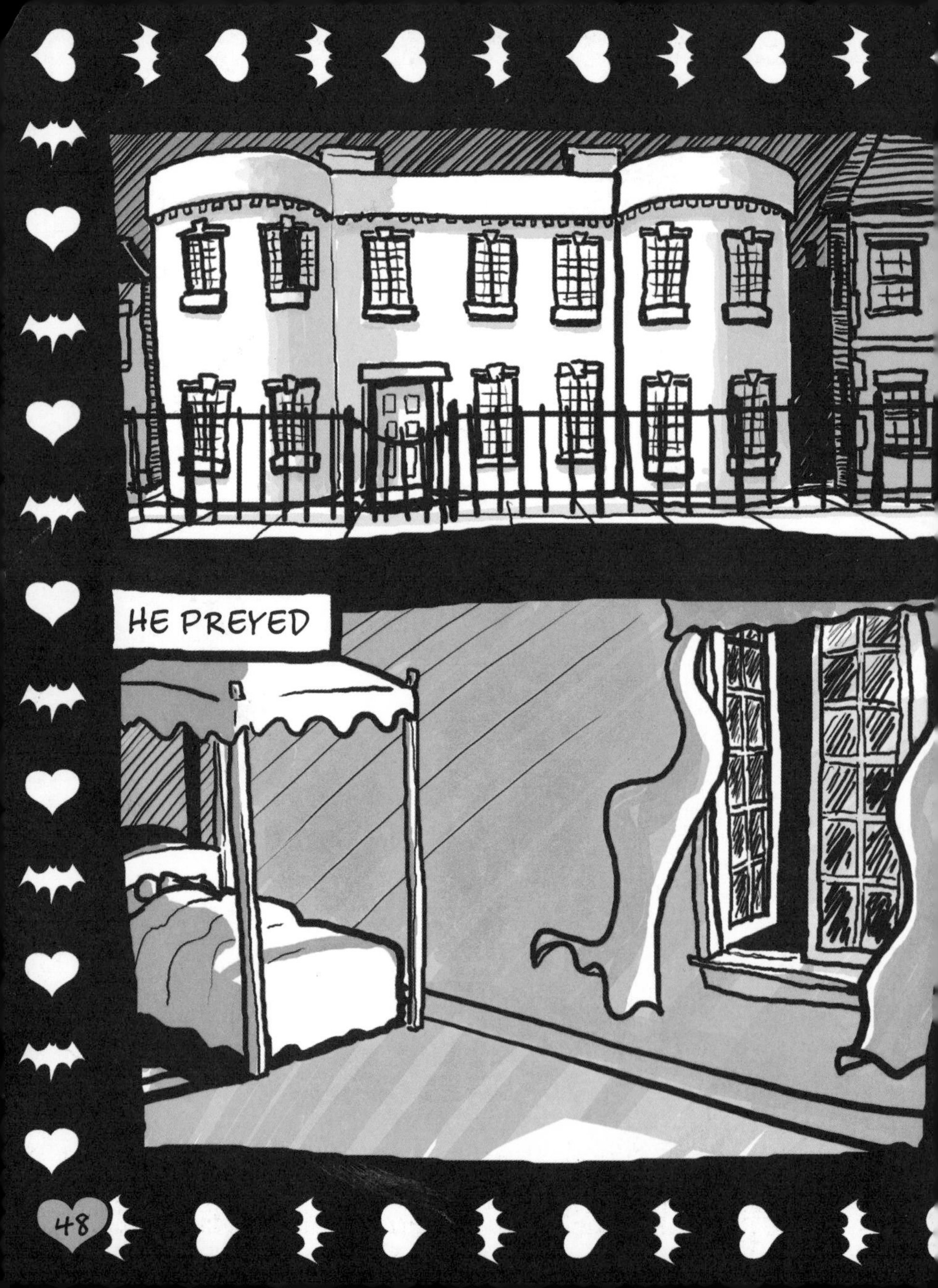
HE PREYED

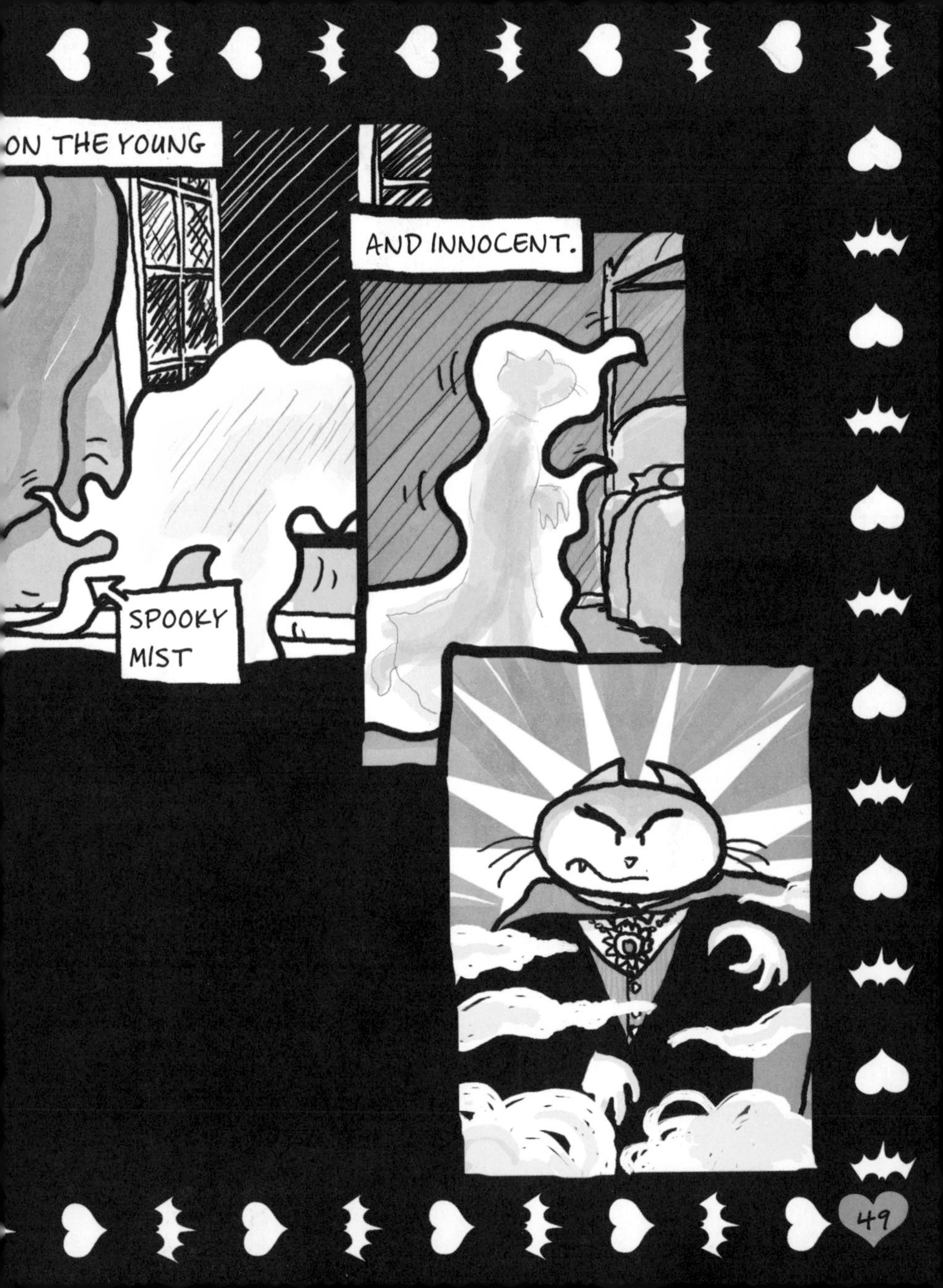
ON THE YOUNG
SPOOKY MIST
AND INNOCENT.

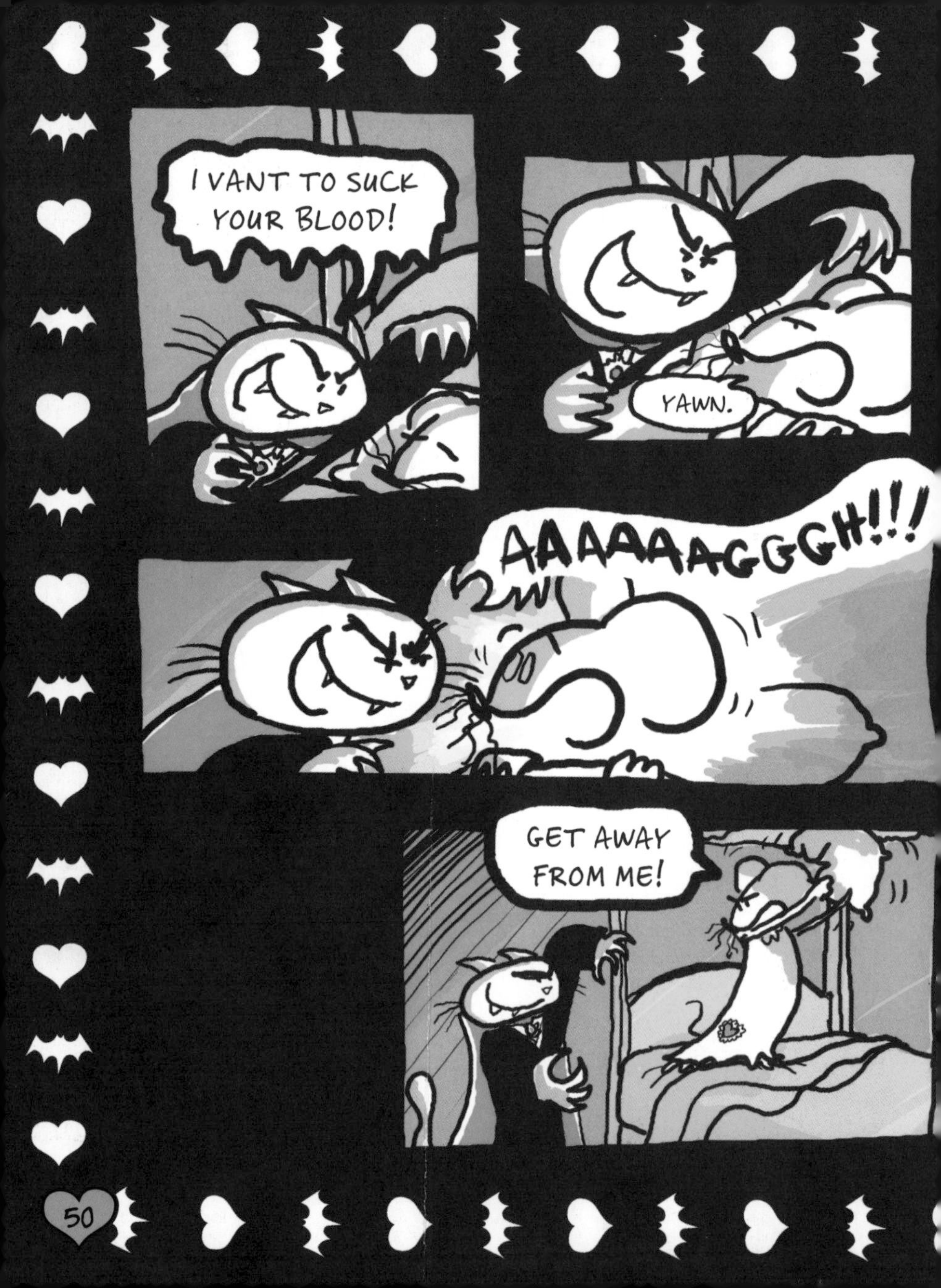
I VANT TO SUCK YOUR BLOOD!
YAWN.
AAAAAAGGGH!!!
GET AWAY FROM ME!

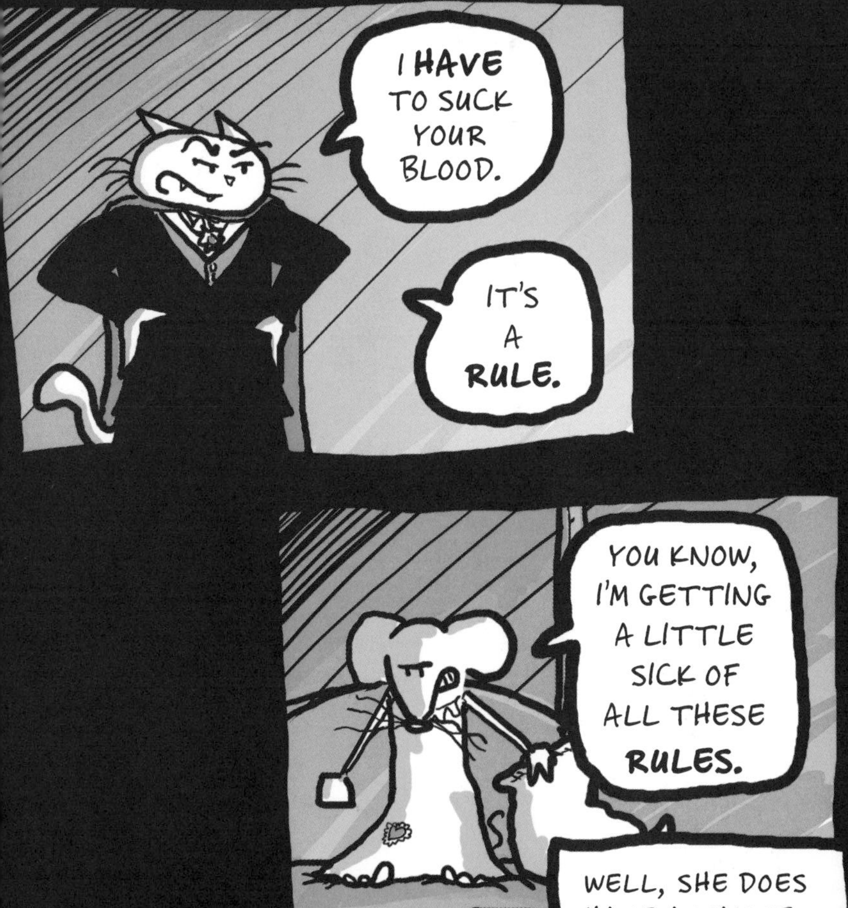
I HAVE TO SUCK YOUR BLOOD.
IT'S A RULE.
YOU KNOW, I'M GETTING A LITTLE SICK OF ALL THESE RULES.
WELL, SHE DOES HAVE A WAY OF SUCKING THE FUN OUT OF EVERYTHING.

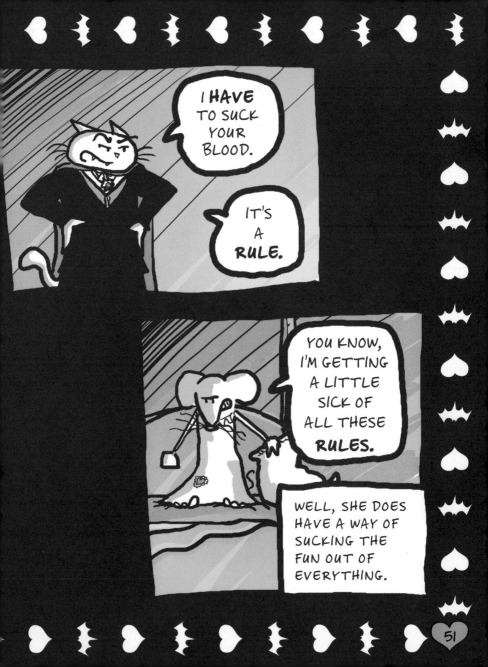

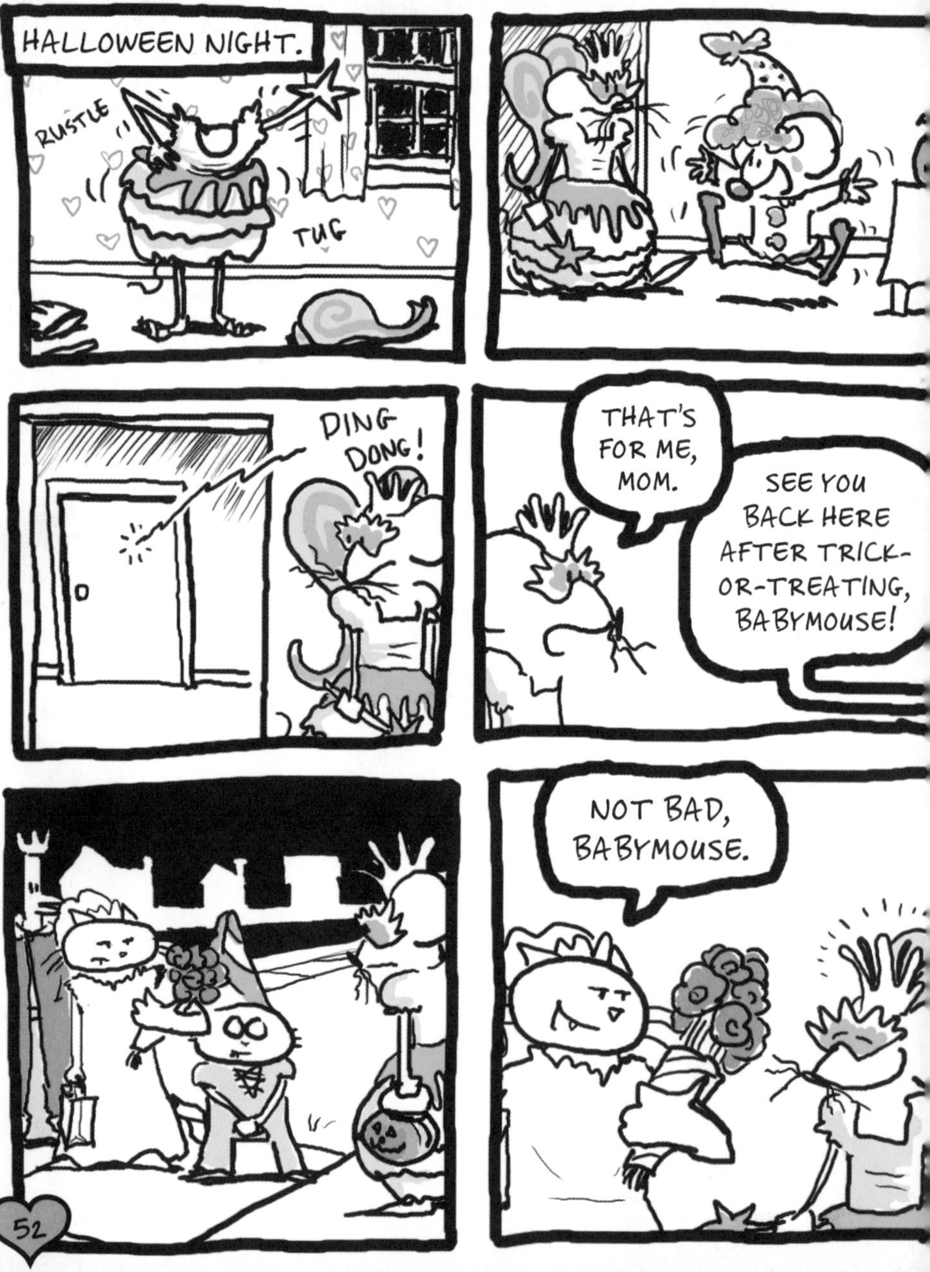
HALLOWEEN NIGHT.
RUSTLE
TUG
DING DONG!
THAT'S FOR ME, MOM.
SEE YOU BACK HERE AFTER TRICK-OR-TREATING, BABYMOUSE!
NOT BAD, BABYMOUSE.

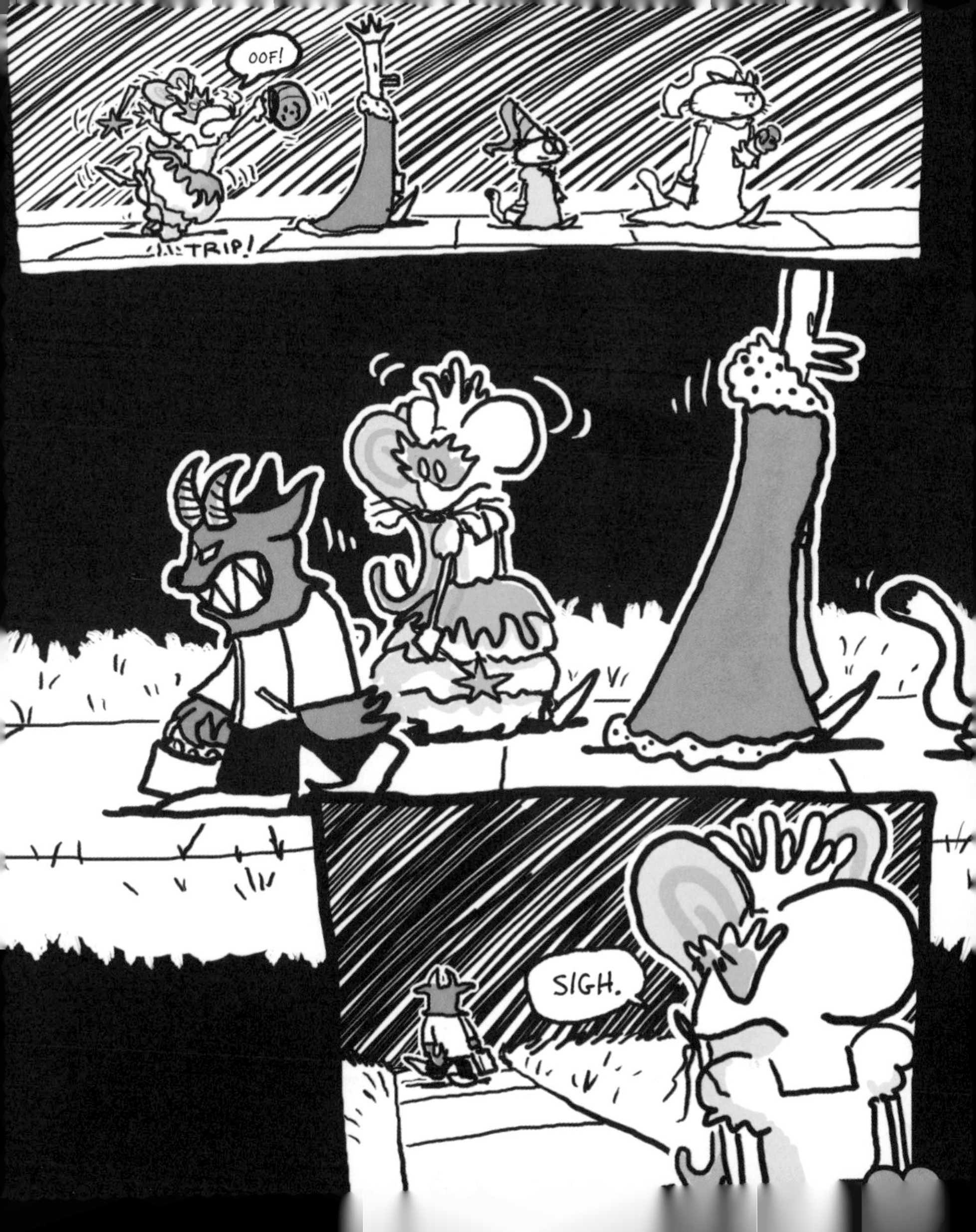
OOF!
TRIP!
SIGH.

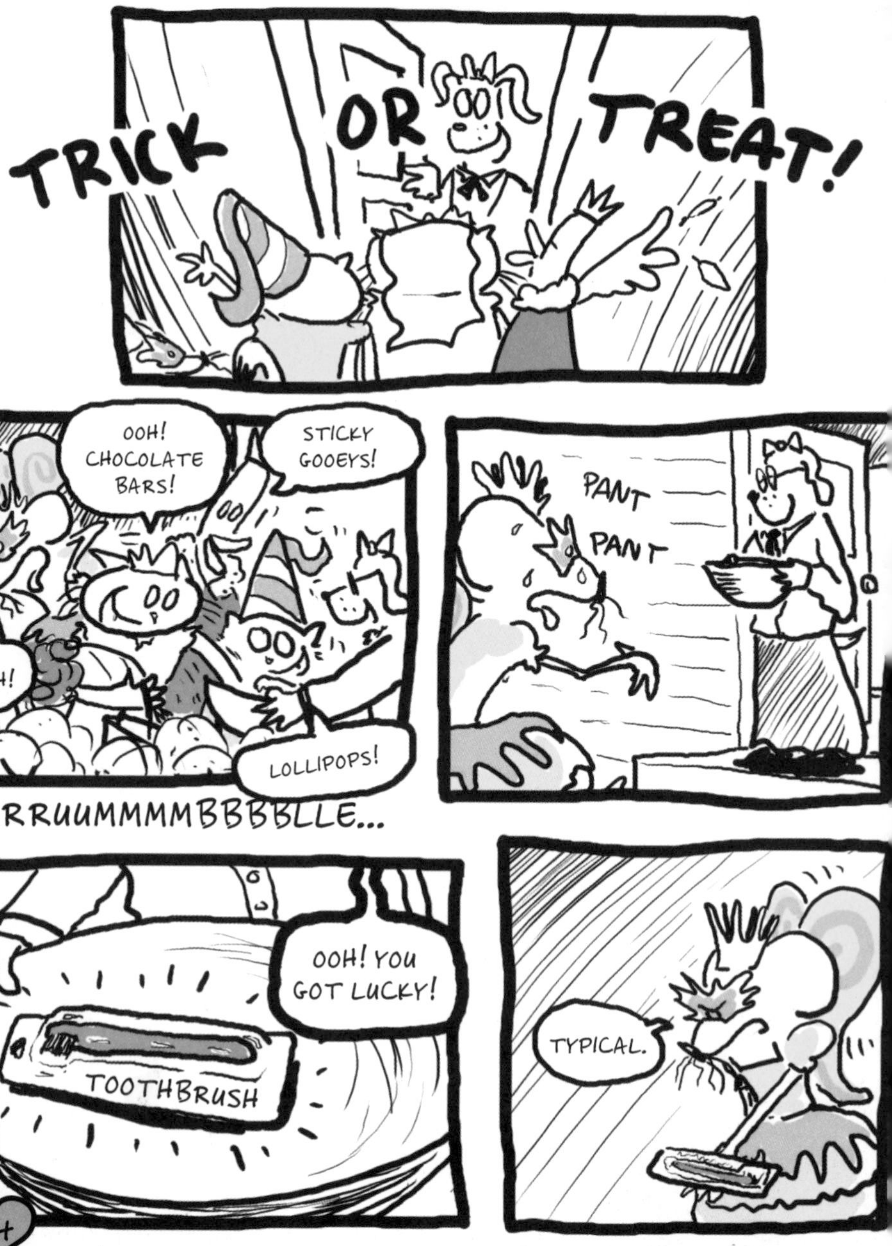
TRICK OR TREAT!
OOH! CHOCOLATE BARS!
STICKY GOOEYS!
UGH!
LOLLIPOPS!
PANT
PANT
RRRUUMMMMBBBBLLE...
OOH! YOU GOT LUCKY!
TOOTHBRUSH
TYPICAL.

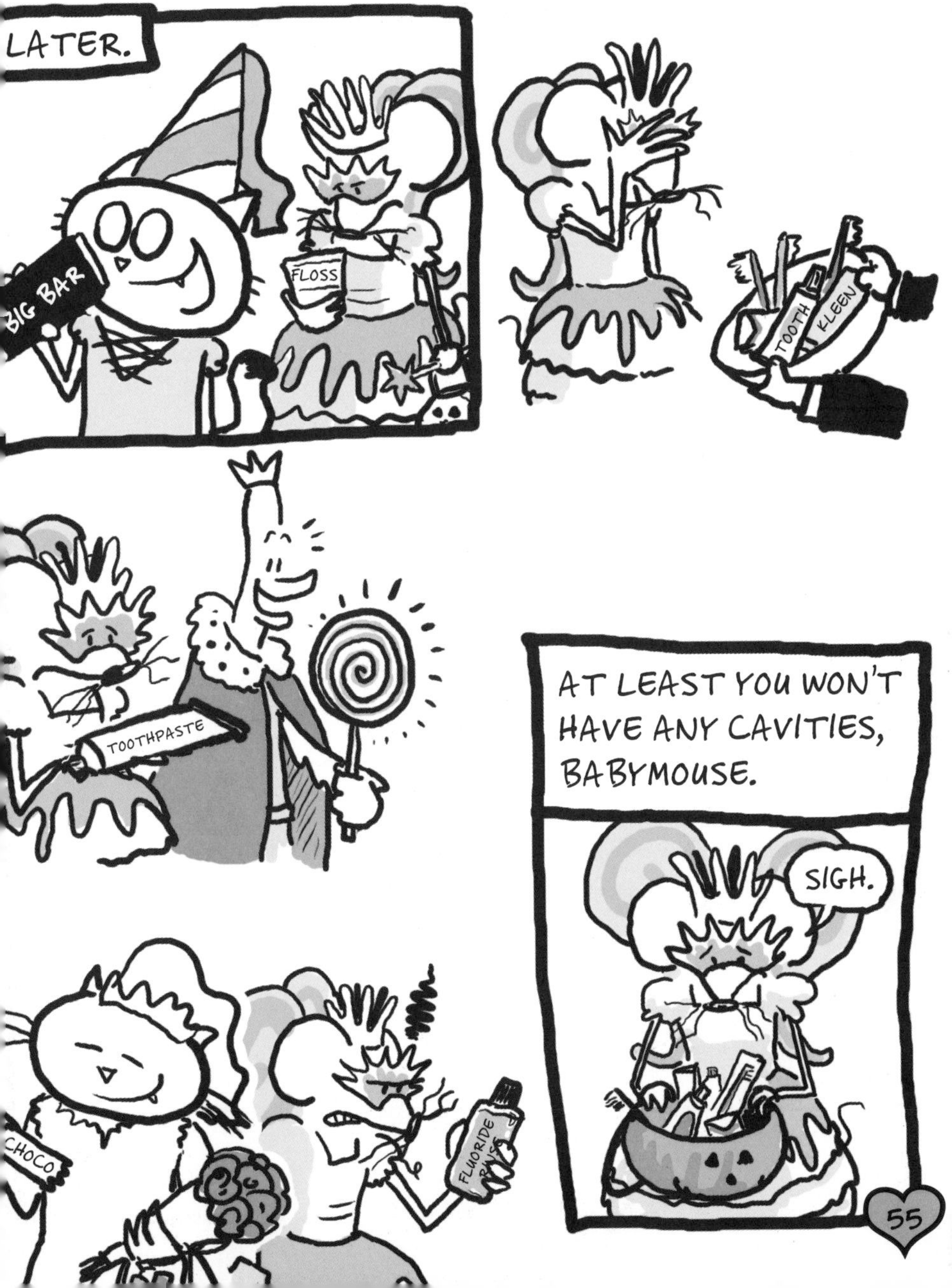

LATER.
BIG BAR
FLOSS
TOOTH
KLEEN
TOOTHPASTE
AT LEAST YOU WON'T HAVE ANY CAVITIES, BABYMOUSE.
SIGH.
CHOCO
FLUORIDE RINSE

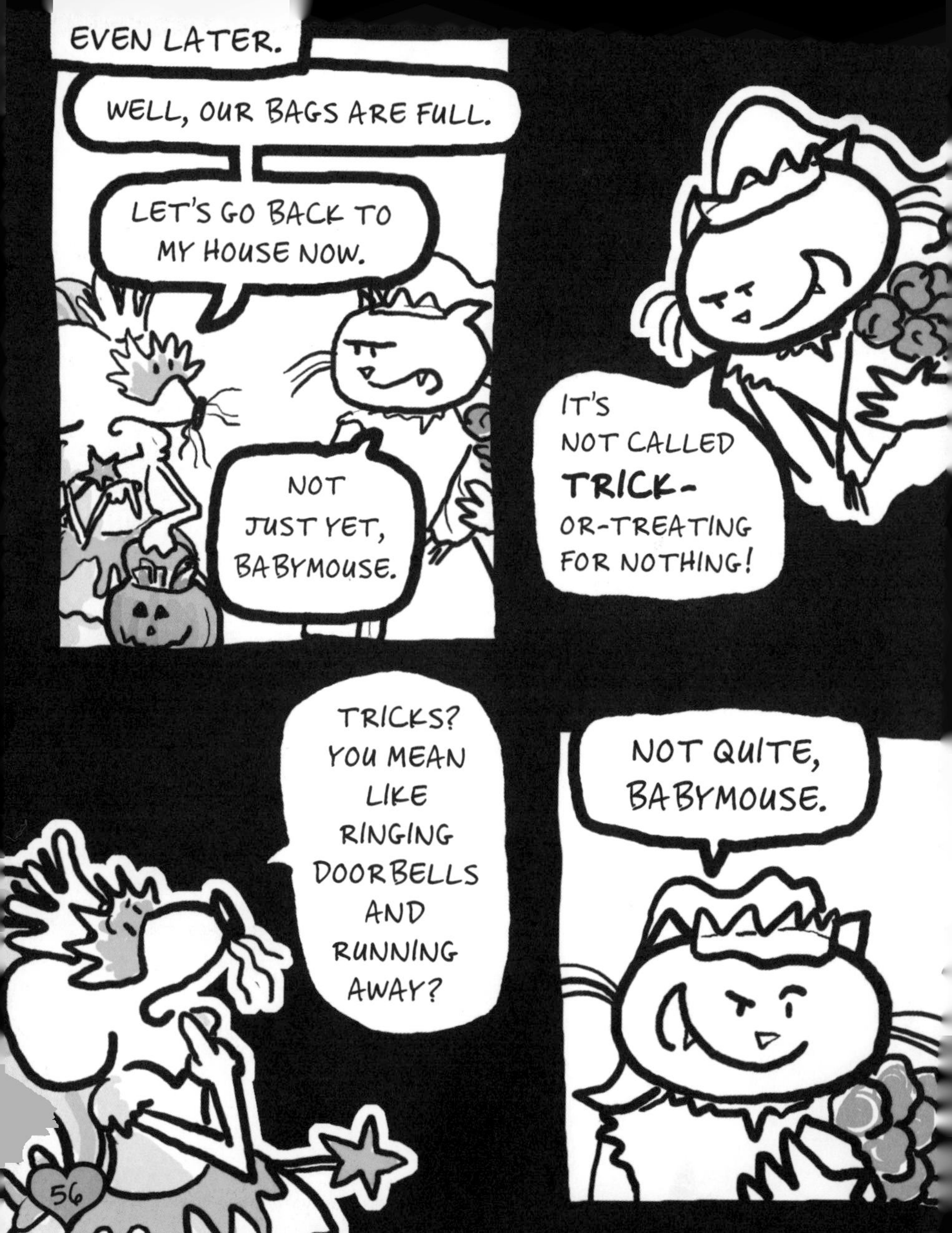
EVEN LATER.
WELL, OUR BAGS ARE FULL.
LET'S GO BACK TO MY HOUSE NOW.
NOT JUST YET, BABYMOUSE.
IT'S NOT CALLED **TRICK-**OR-TREATING FOR NOTHING!
TRICKS? YOU MEAN LIKE RINGING DOORBELLS AND RUNNING AWAY?
NOT QUITE, BABYMOUSE.

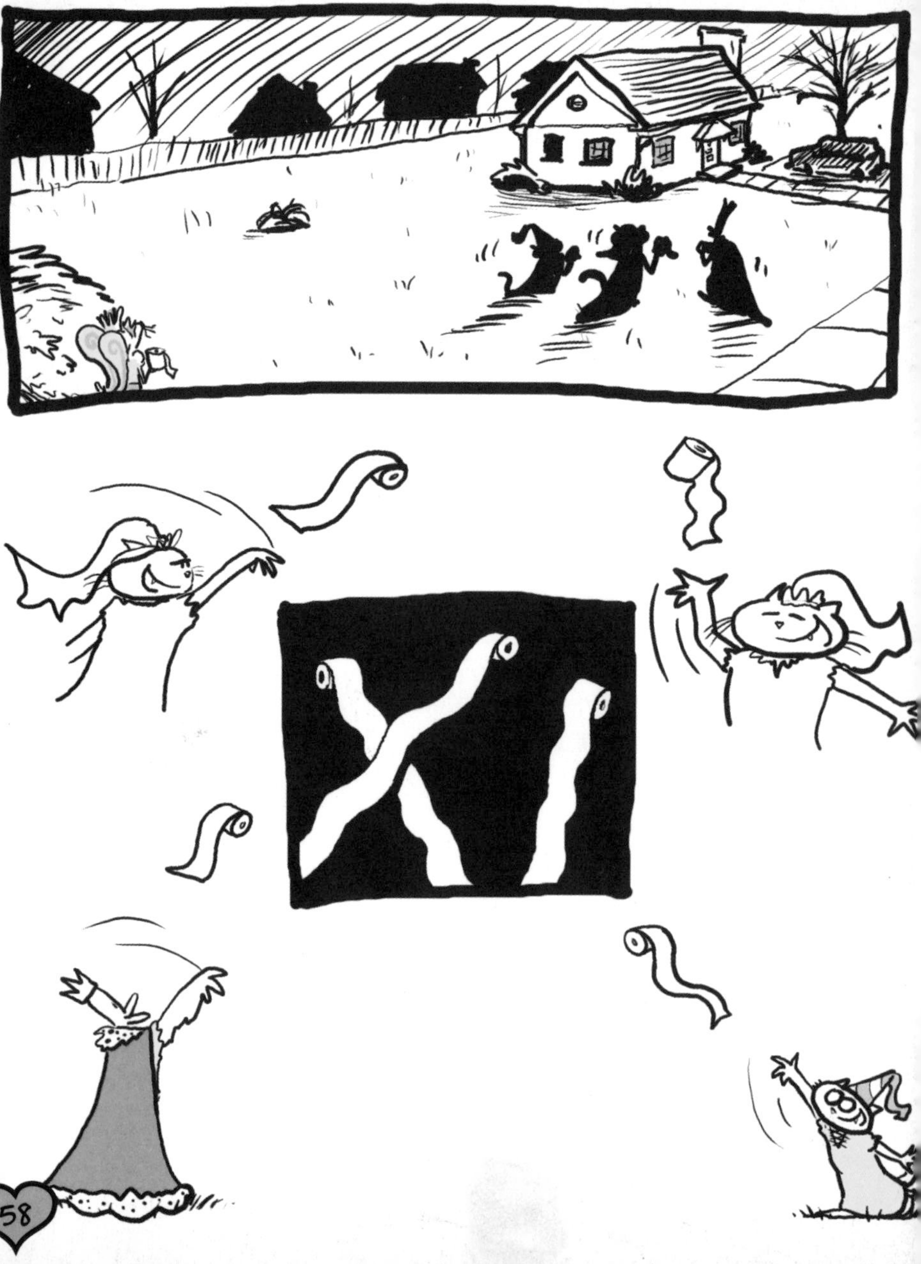

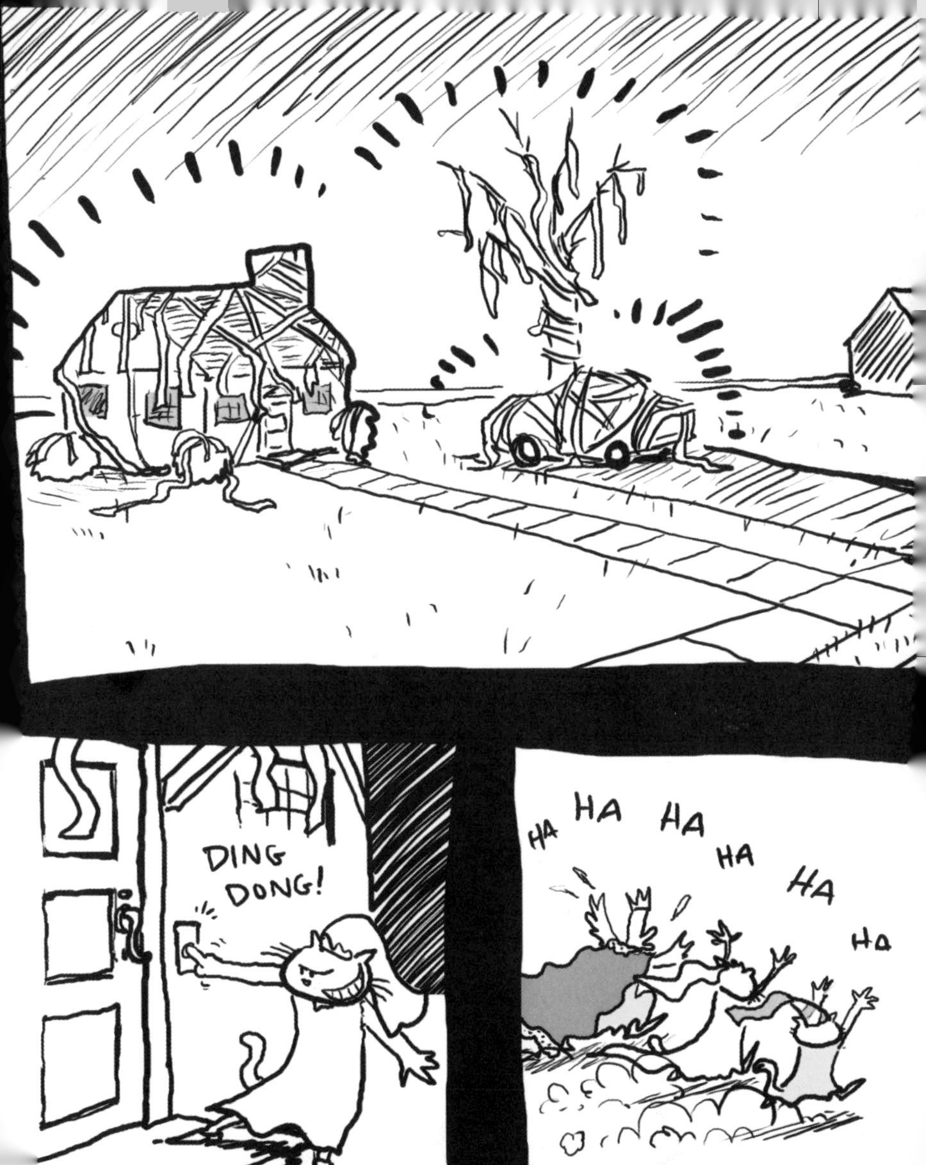
DING DONG!
HA HA HA HA HA HA

R TURN, BABYMOUSE. THAT HOUSE OVER THERE.

TIP TOE TIP TOE TIP TOE

GULP!

BABYMOUSE— THINK OF THE TREES. BESIDES, WASTING TOILET PAPER LIKE THAT ISN'T VERY GOOD FOR THE ENVIRONMENT.

I KNOW.

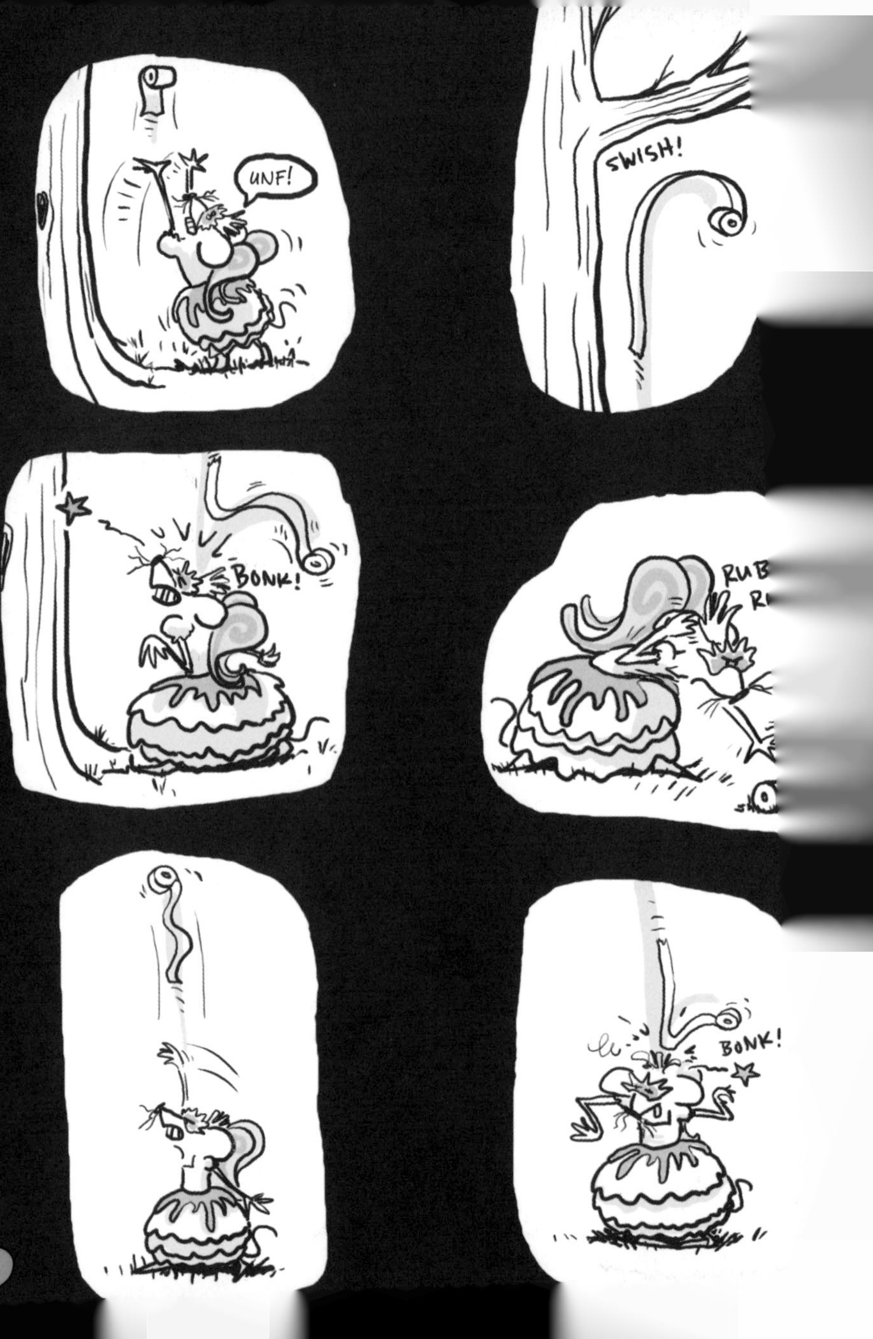
UNF!
SWISH!
BONK!
BONK!

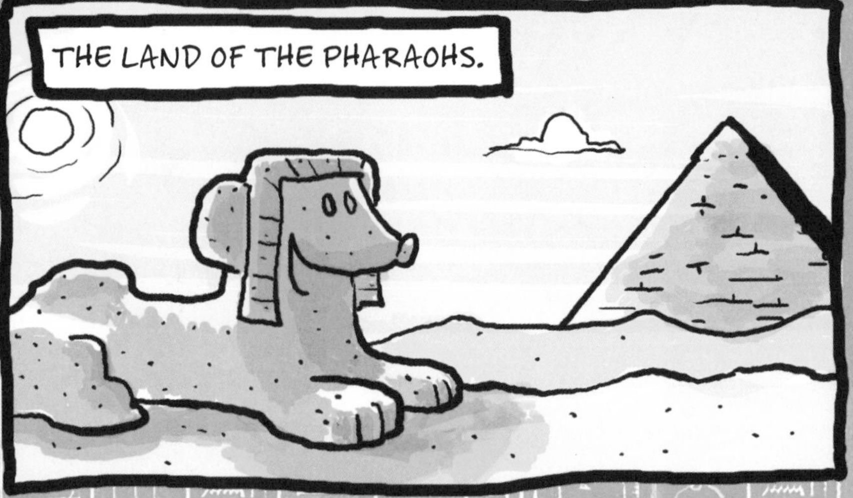
THE LAND OF THE PHARAOHS.

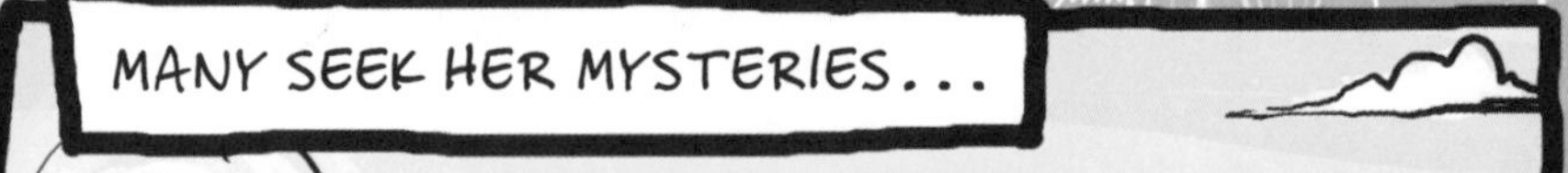
MANY SEEK HER MYSTERIES...

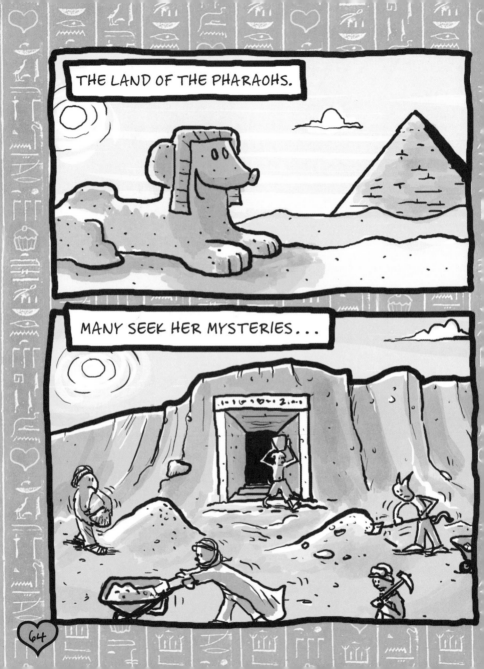

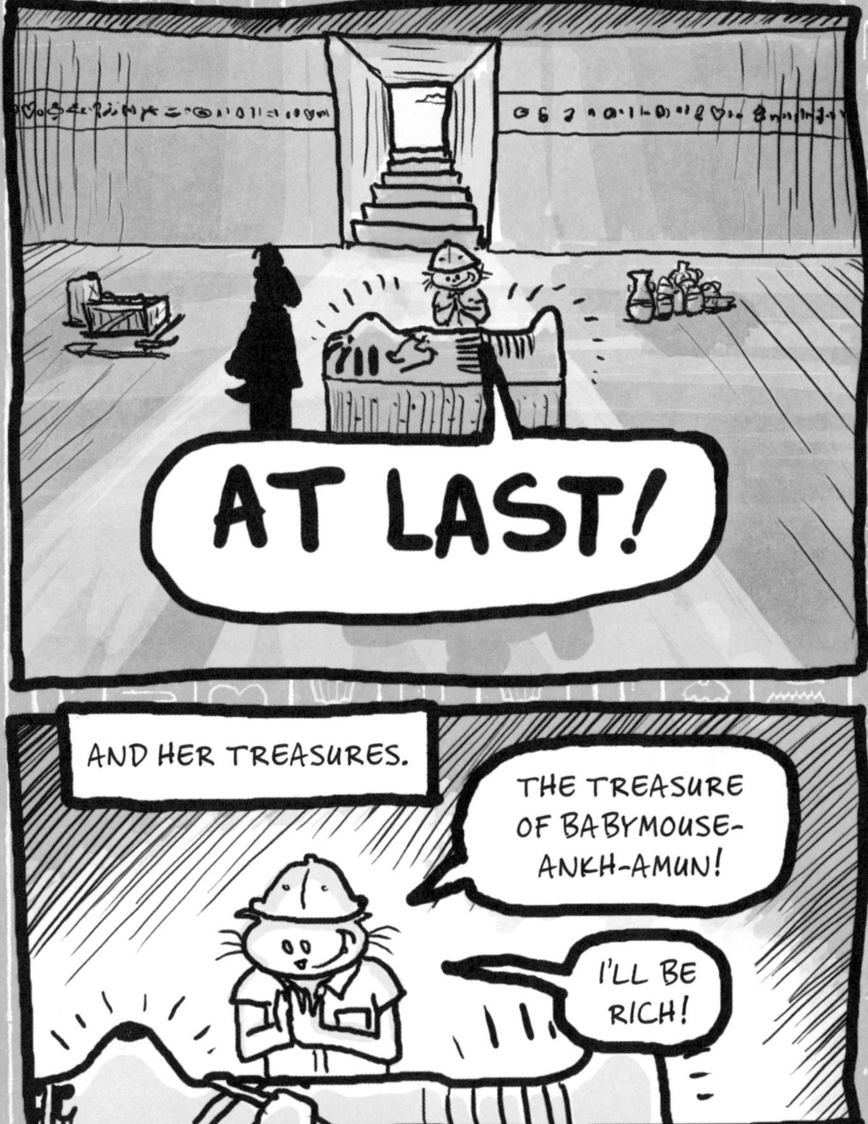
AT LAST!
AND HER TREASURES.
THE TREASURE OF BABYMOUSE-ANKH-AMUN!
I'LL BE RICH!

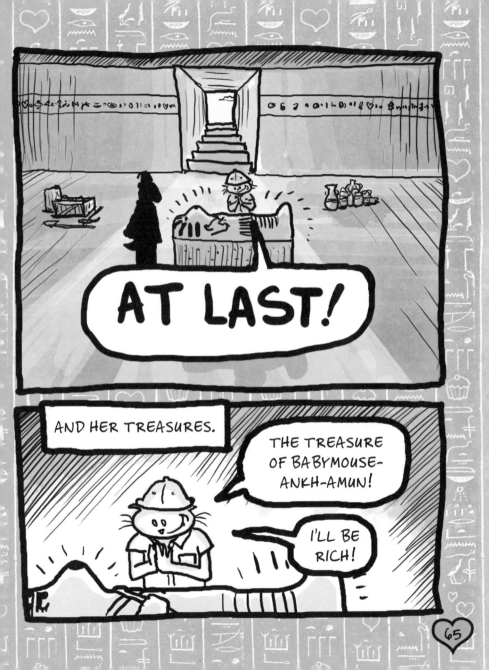

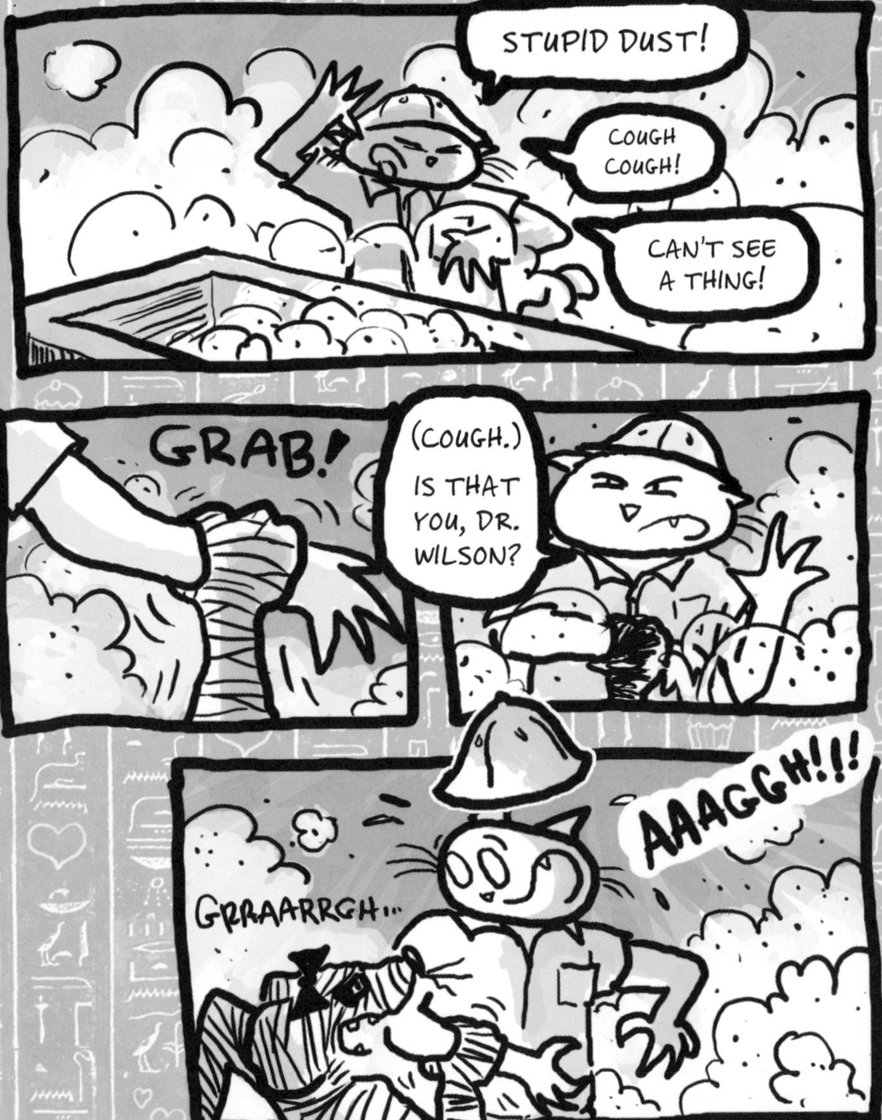
STUPID DUST!
COUGH COUGH!
CAN'T SEE A THING!
GRAB!
(COUGH.) IS THAT YOU, DR. WILSON?
AAAGGH!!!
GRRAARRGH...

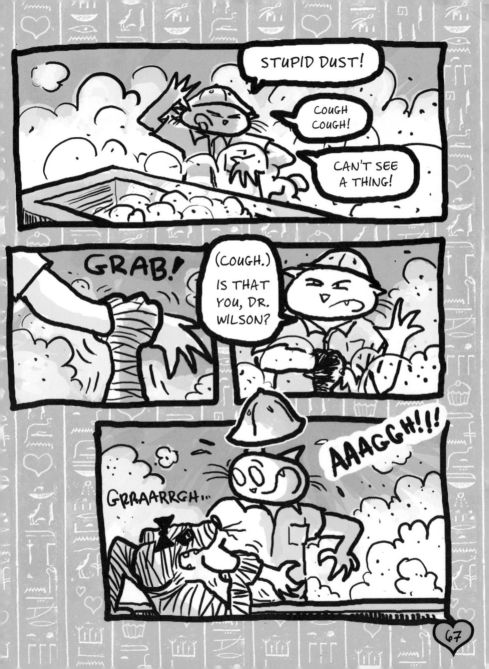

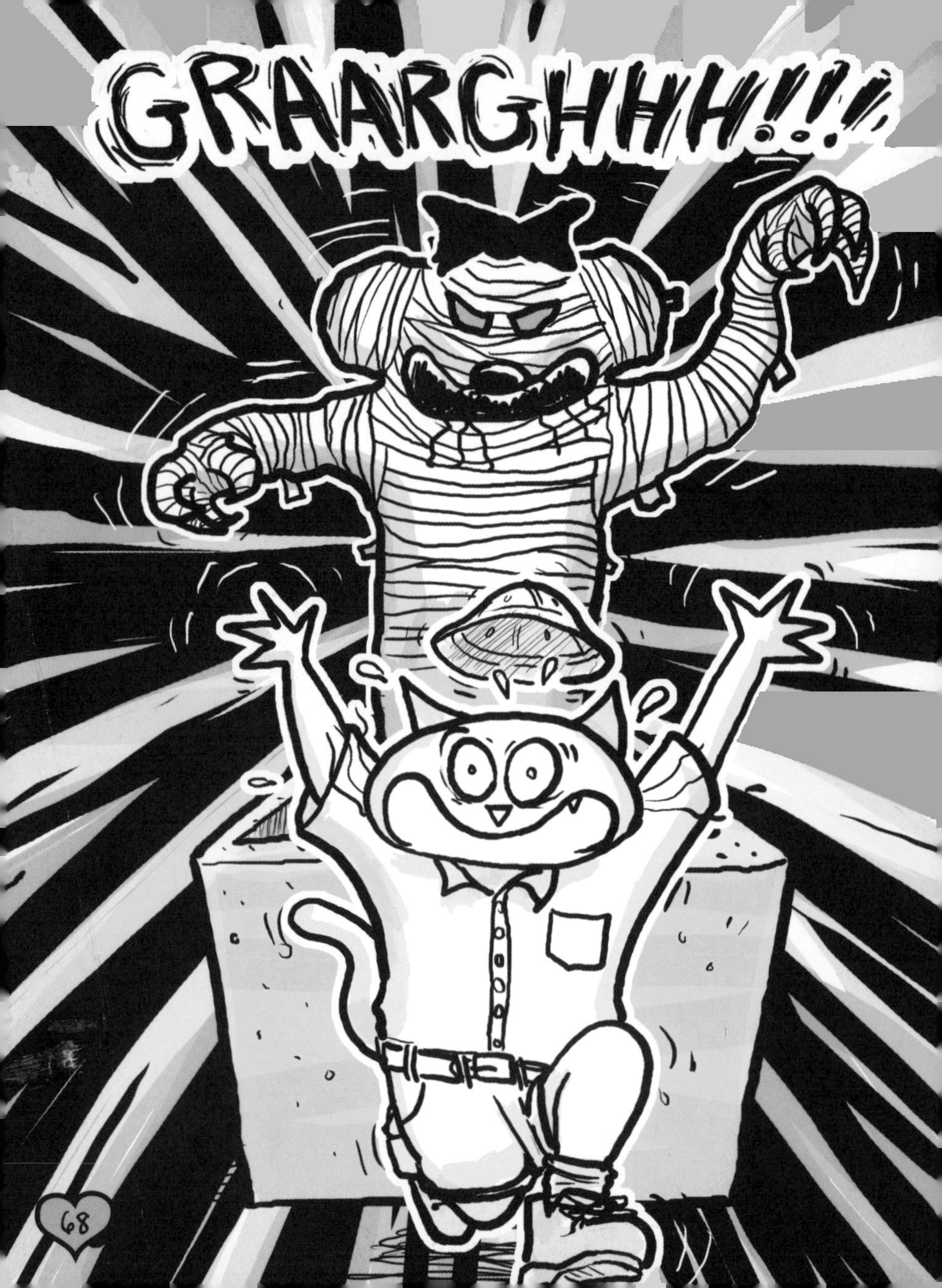
GRAARGHHHH!!!

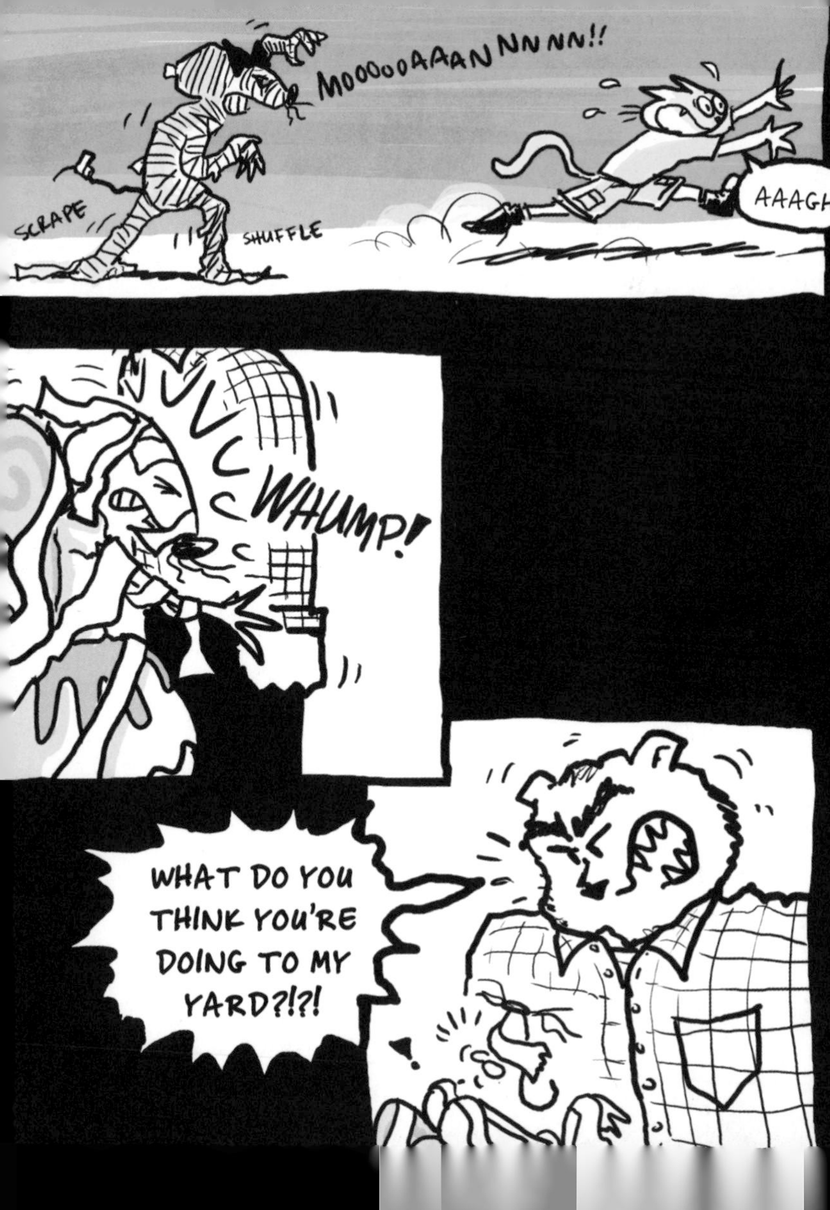
MOOOOOAAANNNNN!!
SCRAPE
SHUFFLE
AAAGH!
WHUMP!
WHAT DO YOU THINK YOU'RE DOING TO MY YARD?!?!

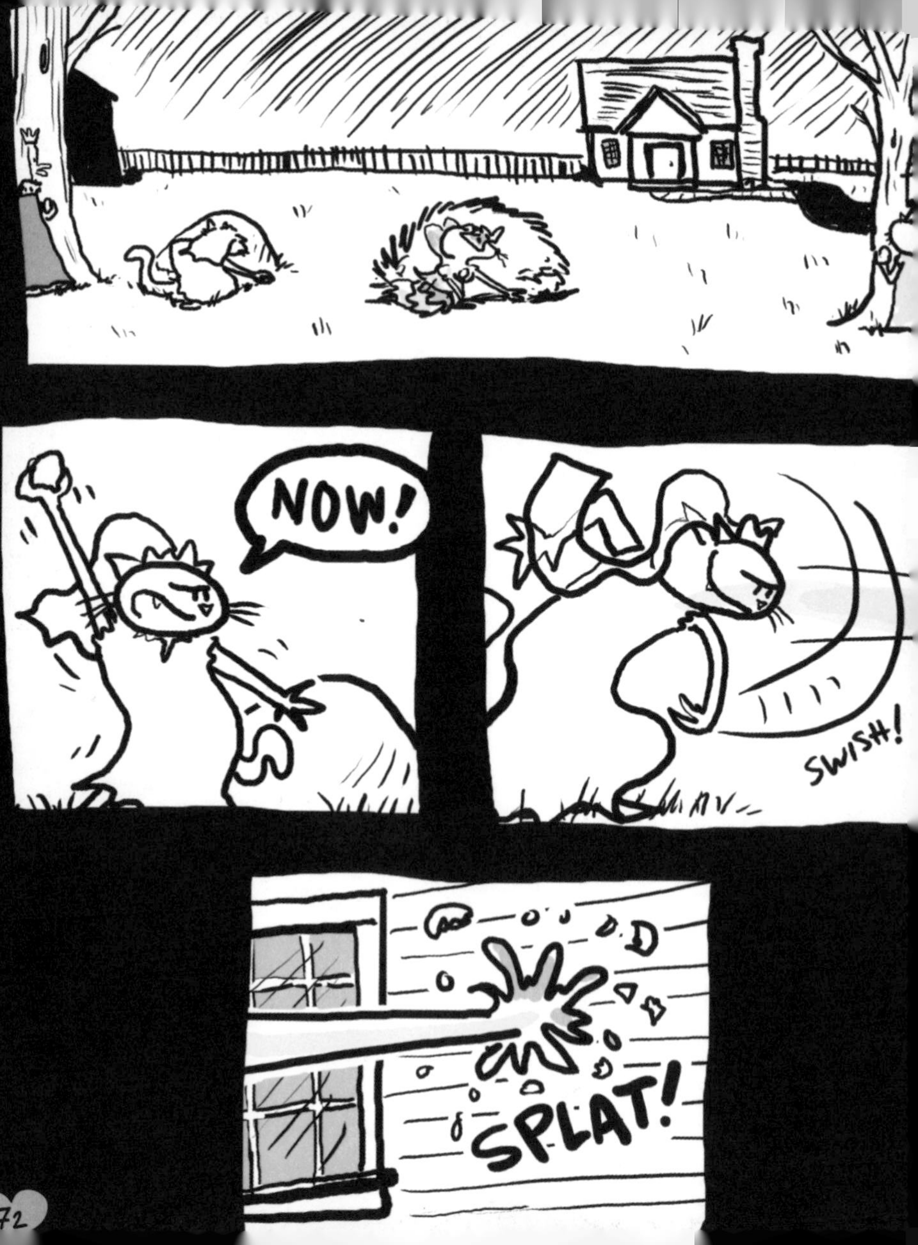
NOW!
SWISH!
SPLAT!

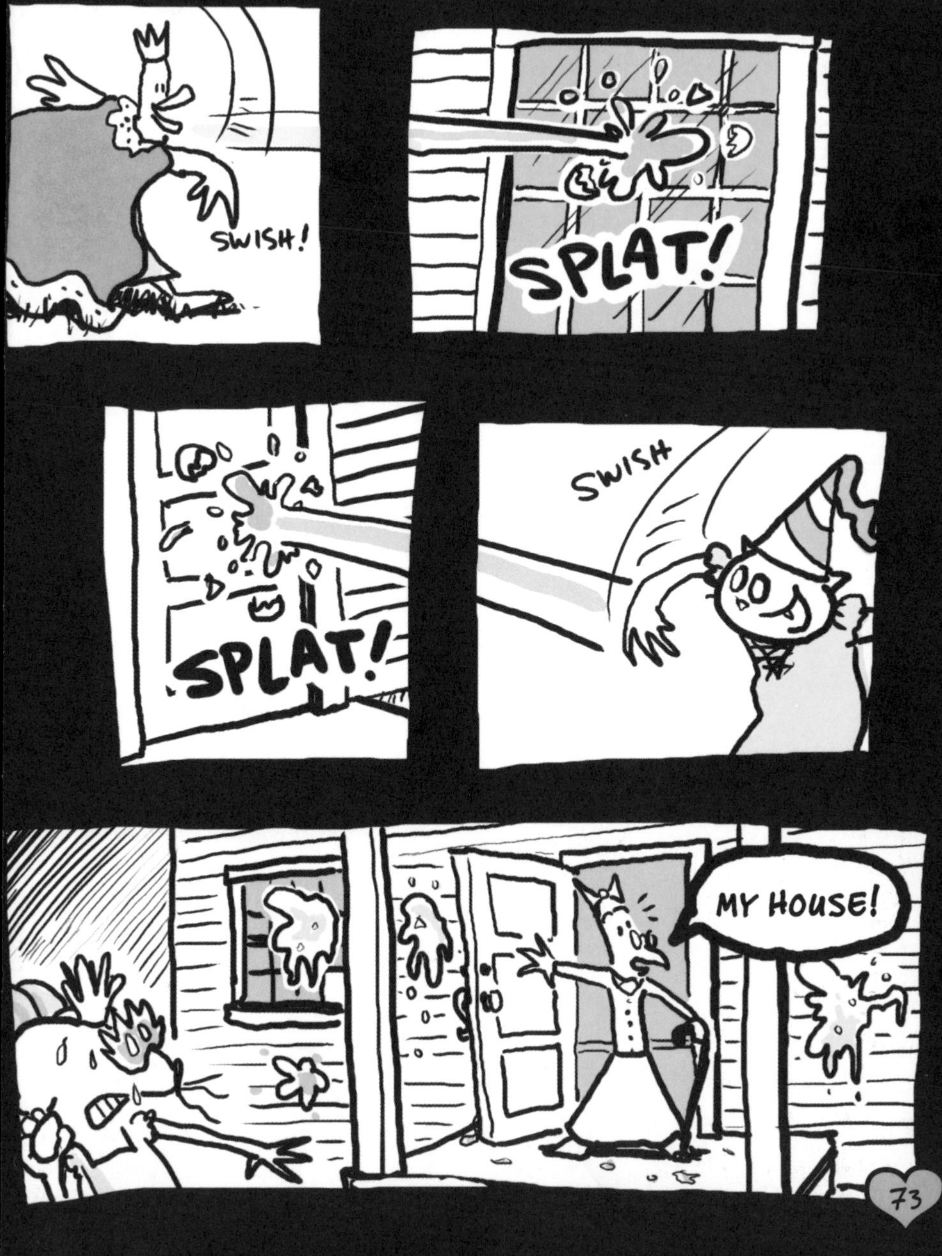
SWISH!
SPLAT!
SPLAT!
SWISH
MY HOUSE!

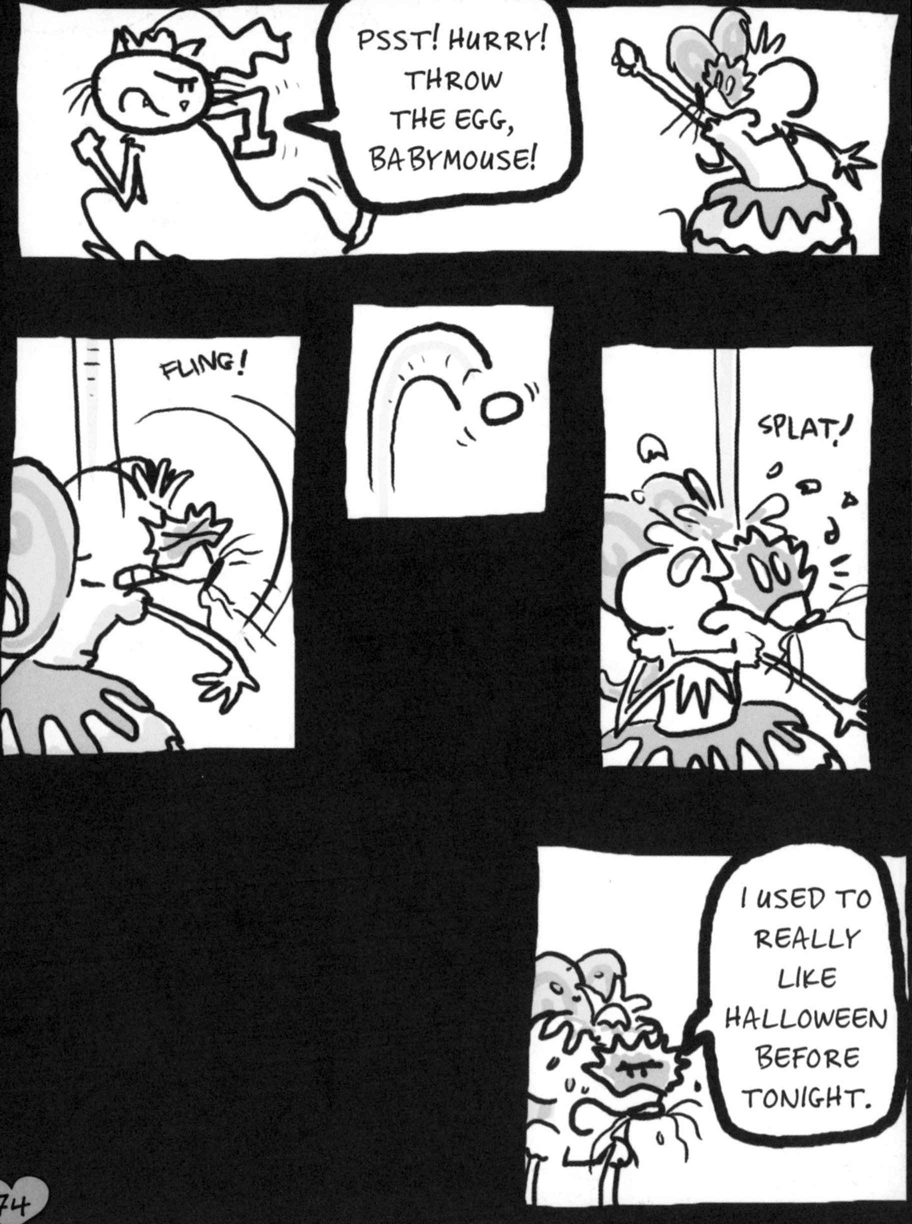
PSST! HURRY! THROW THE EGG, BABYMOUSE!
FLING!
SPLAT!
I USED TO REALLY LIKE HALLOWEEN BEFORE TONIGHT.

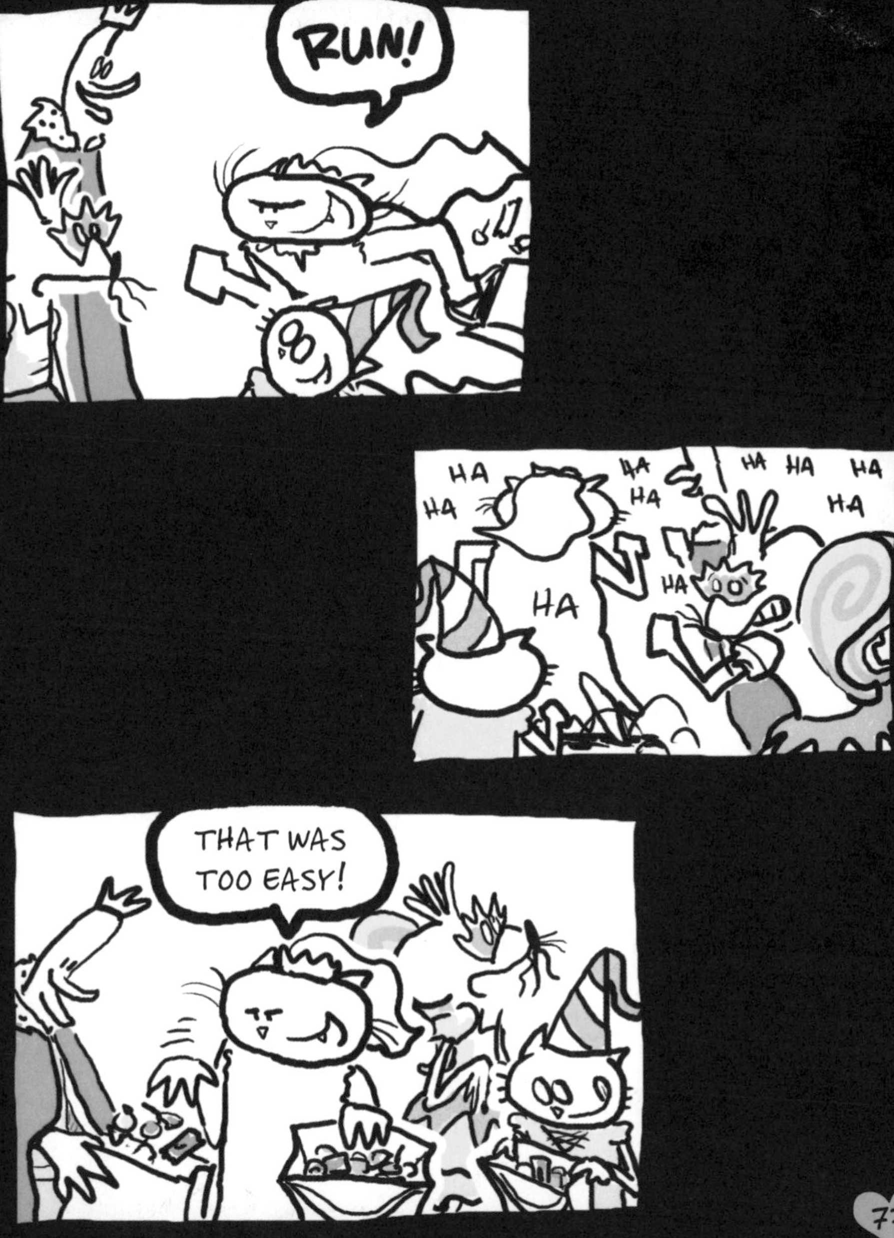
RUN!
HA HA HA HA HA HA HA HA
HA
HA
THAT WAS TOO EASY!

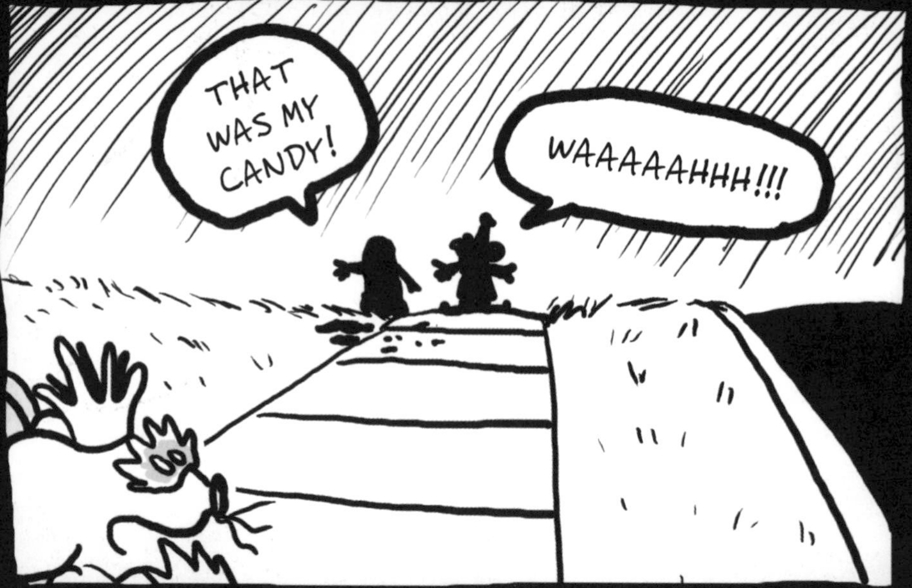
THAT WAS MY CANDY!
WAAAAAAHHH!!!

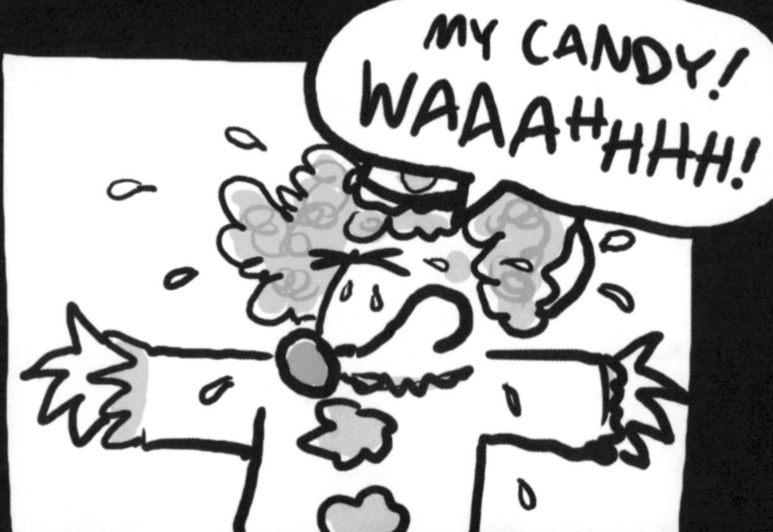
MY CANDY! WAAAHHHH!

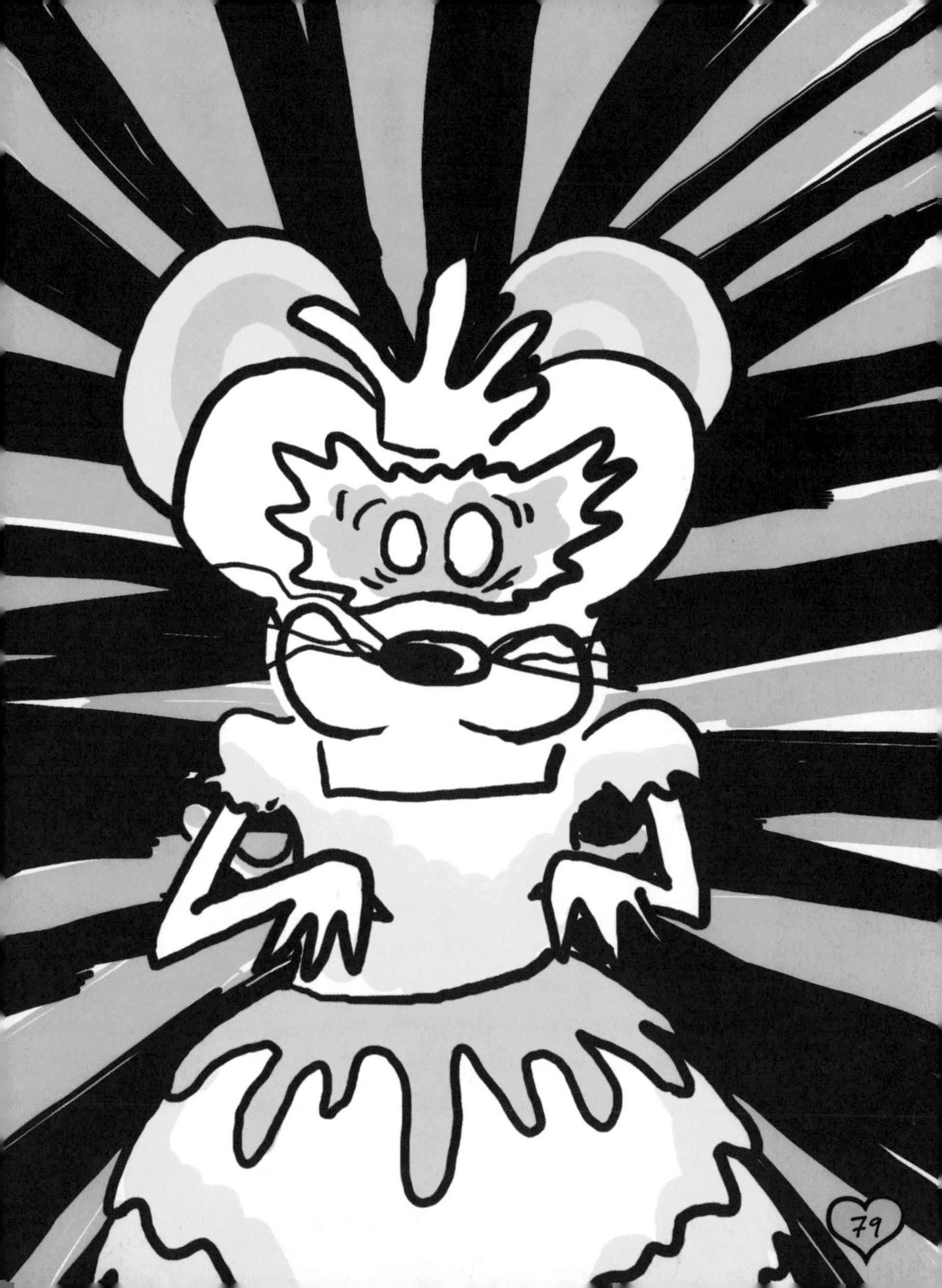

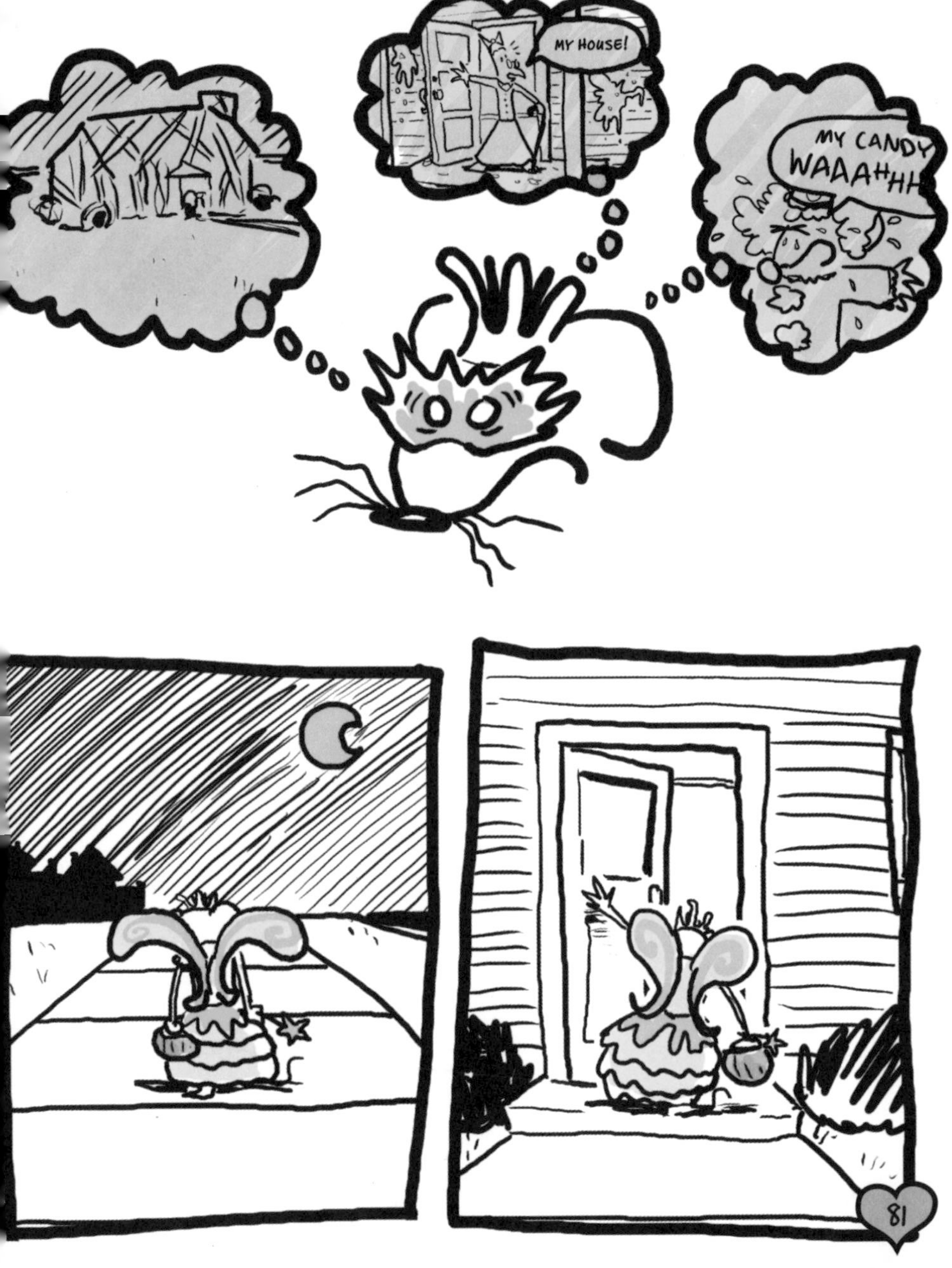
MY HOUSE!
MY CANDY
WAAAHHH

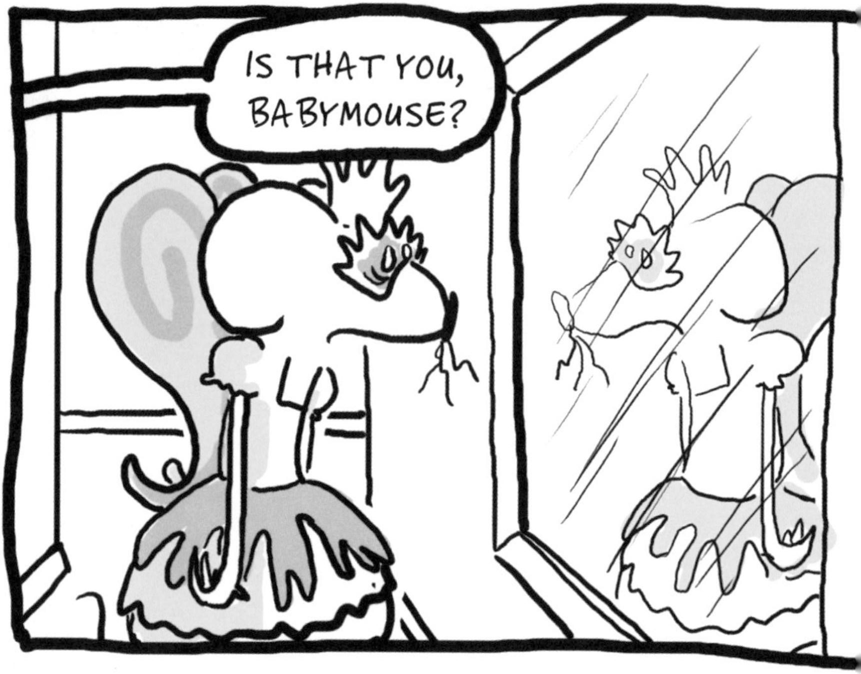
IS THAT YOU, BABYMOUSE?

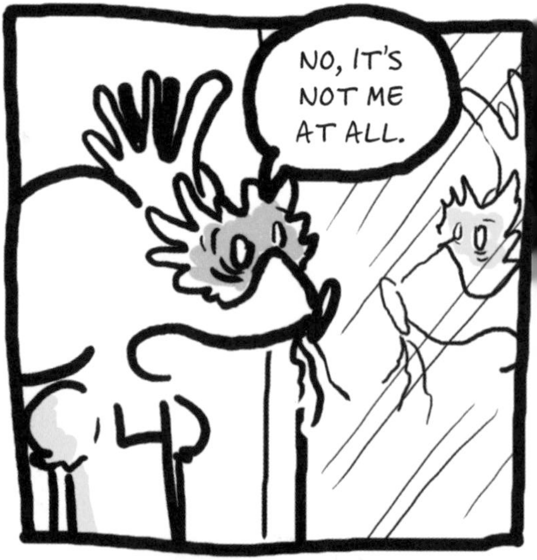
NO, IT'S NOT ME AT ALL.

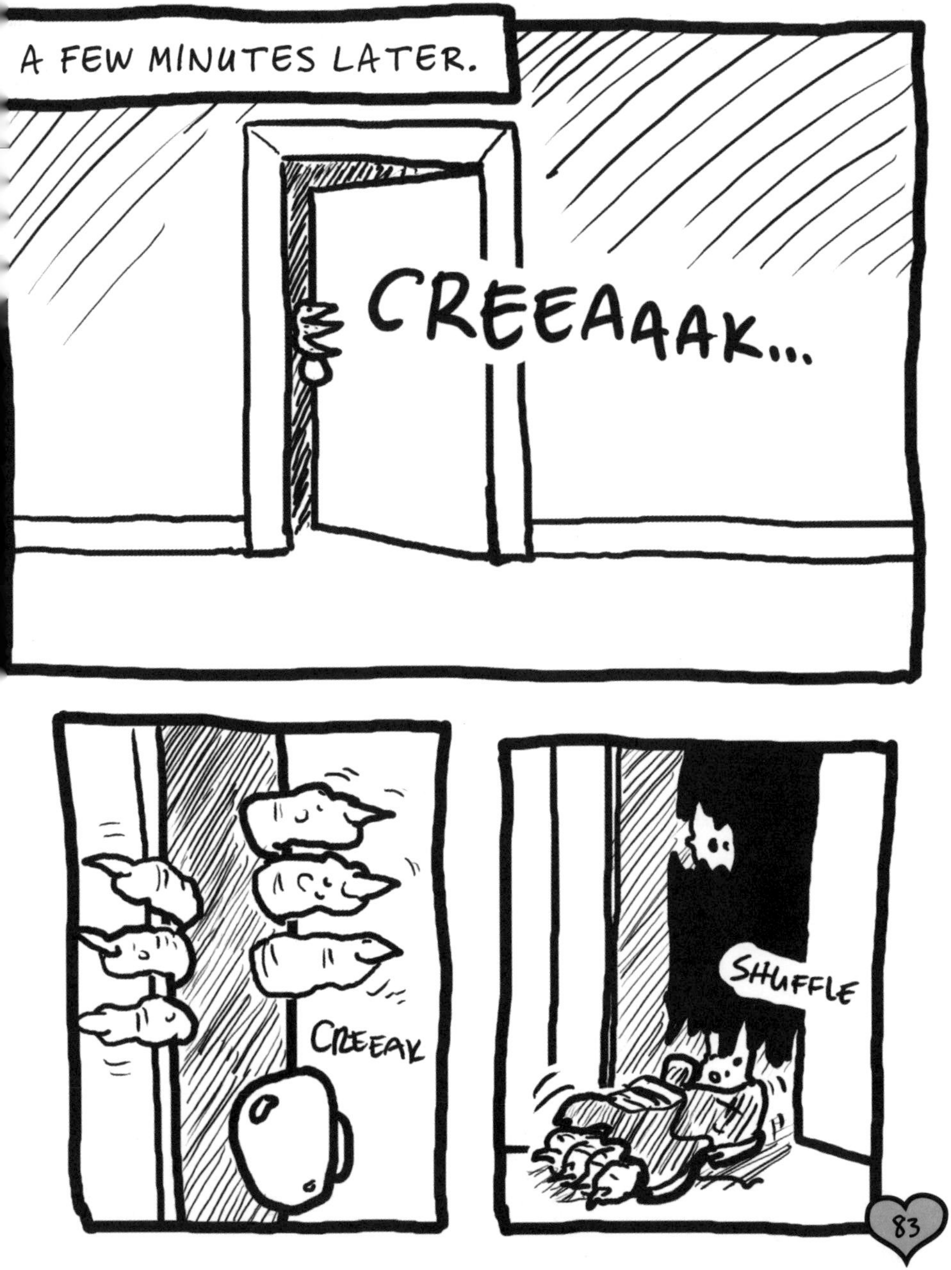
A FEW MINUTES LATER.
CREEAAAK...
CREEAK
SHUFFLE

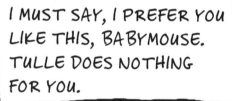

I MUST SAY, I PREFER YOU LIKE THIS, BABYMOUSE. TULLE DOES NOTHING FOR YOU.

THANKS!

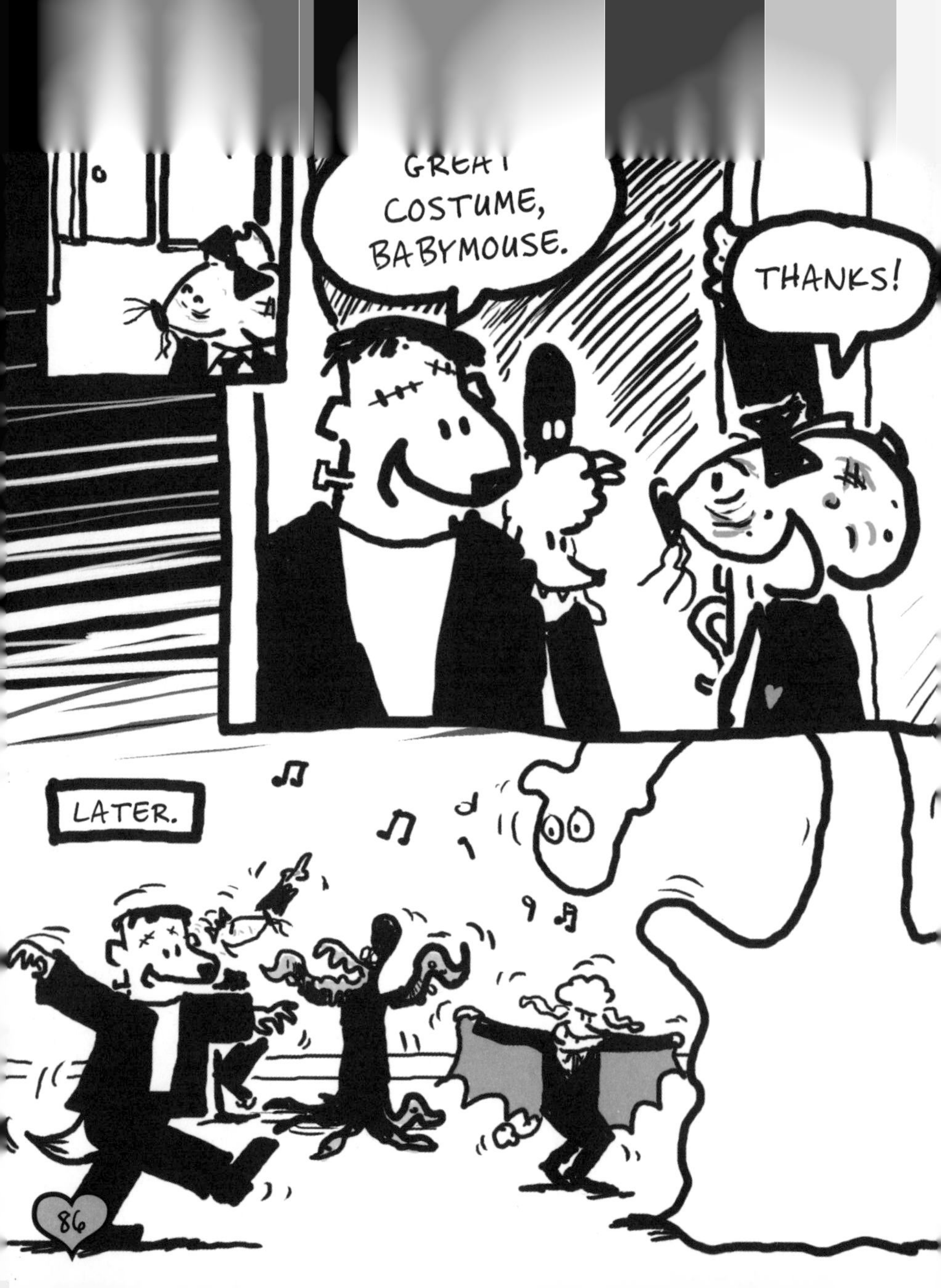
GREAT COSTUME, BABYMOUSE.
THANKS!
LATER.

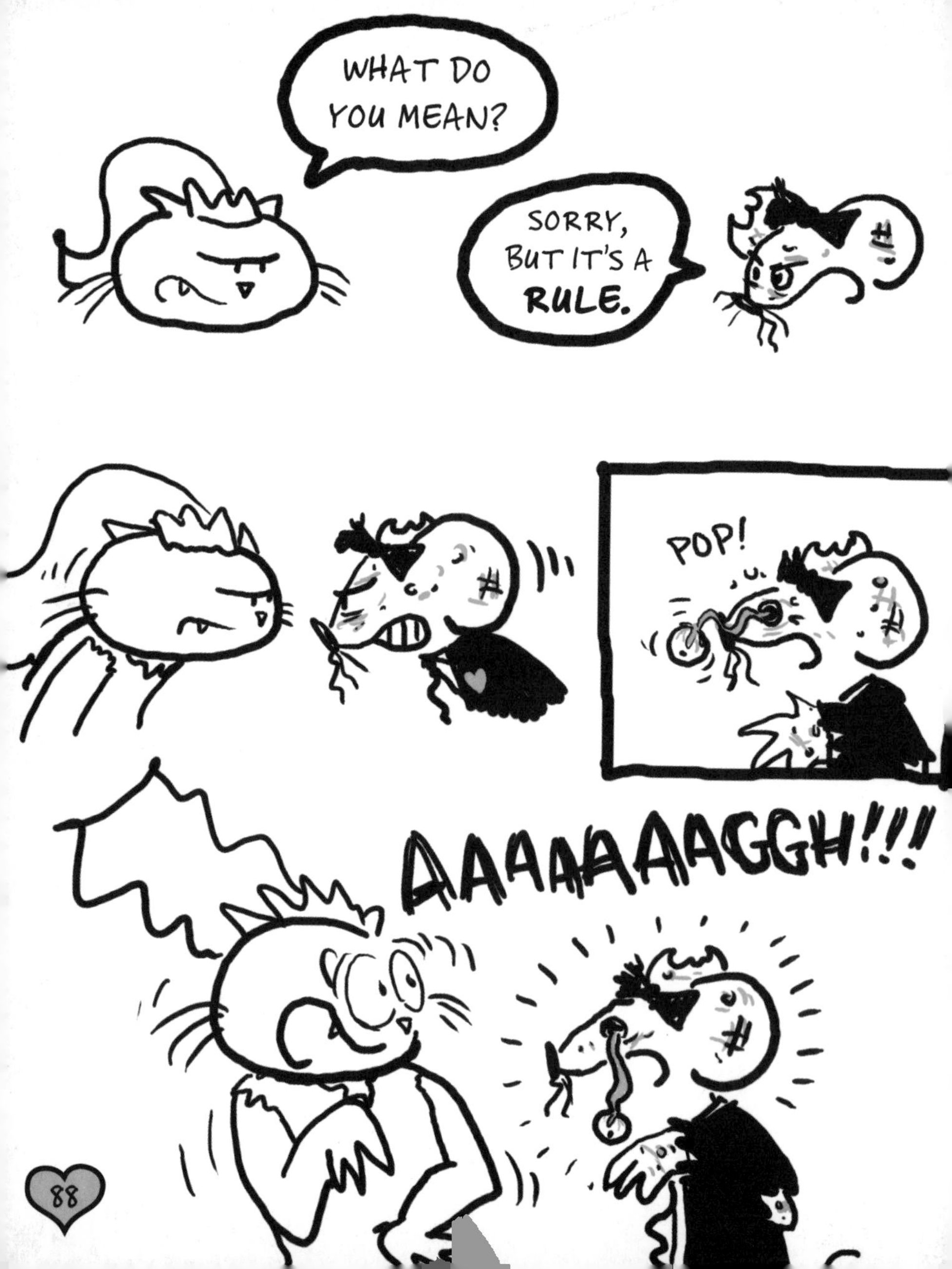
WHAT DO YOU MEAN?
SORRY, BUT IT'S A **RULE.**
POP!
AAAAAAAGGH!!!!

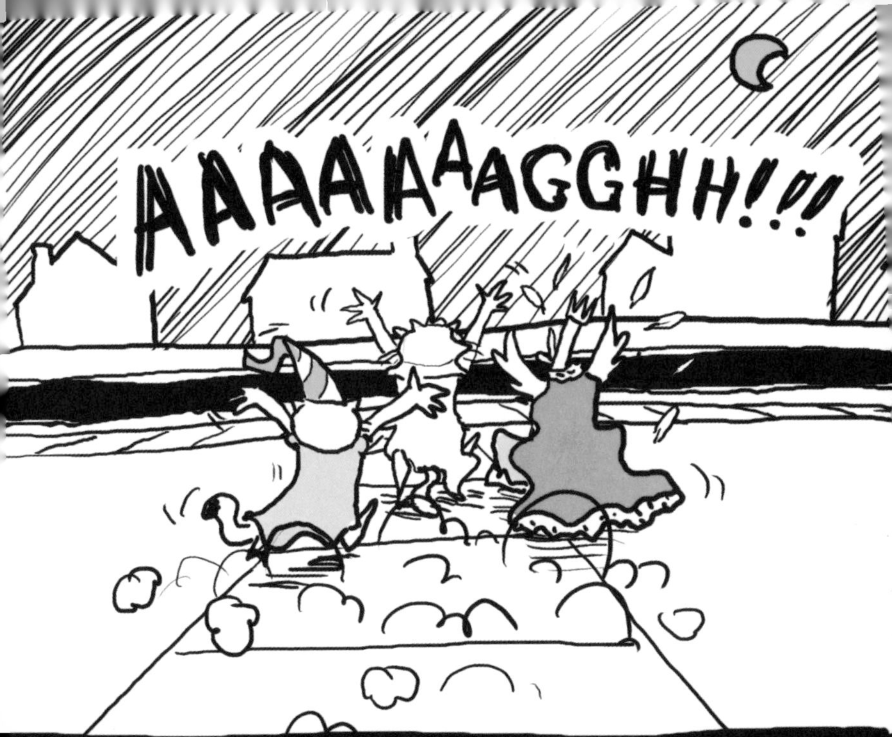
AAAAAAAGGHH!!!!

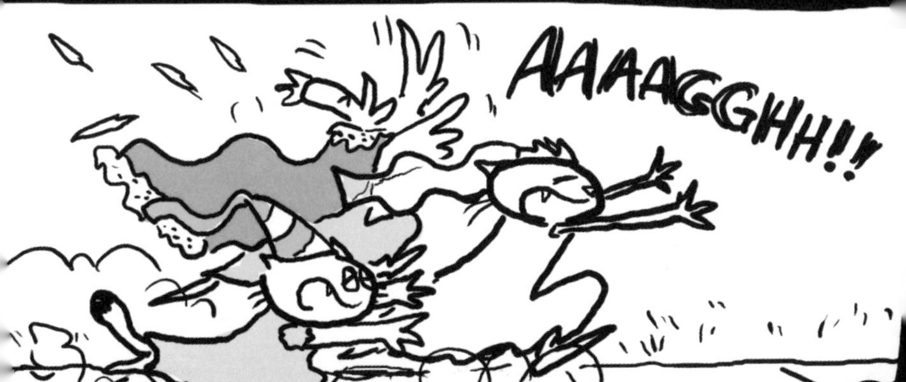
AAAAGGHH!!

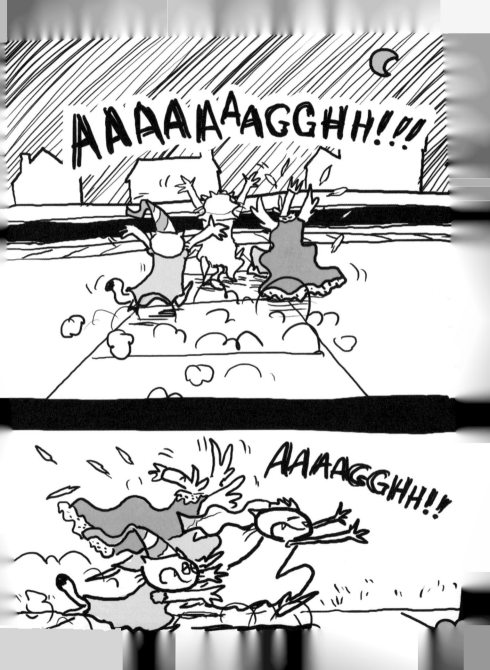

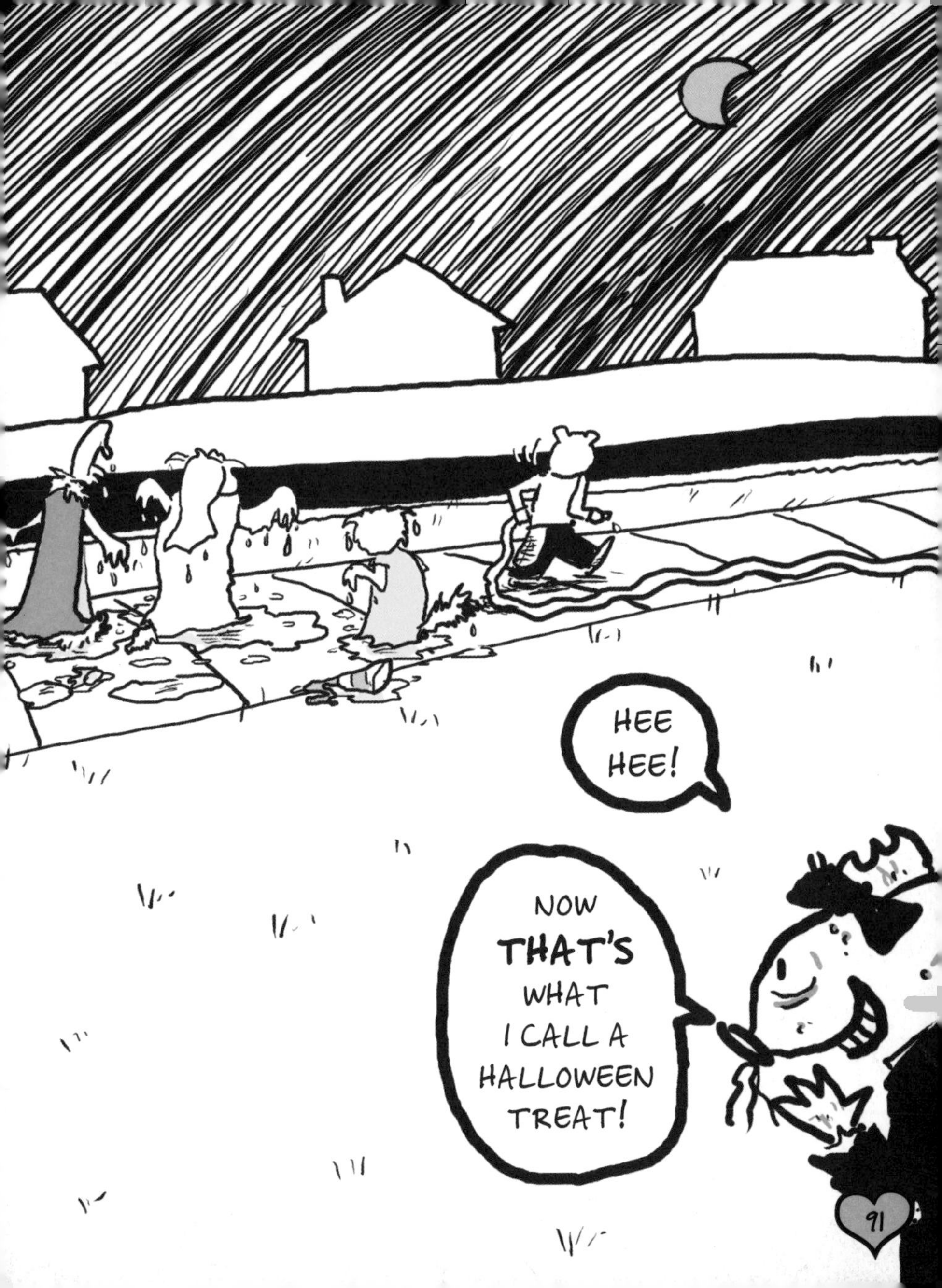
HEE HEE!
NOW THAT'S WHAT I CALL A HALLOWEEN TREAT!

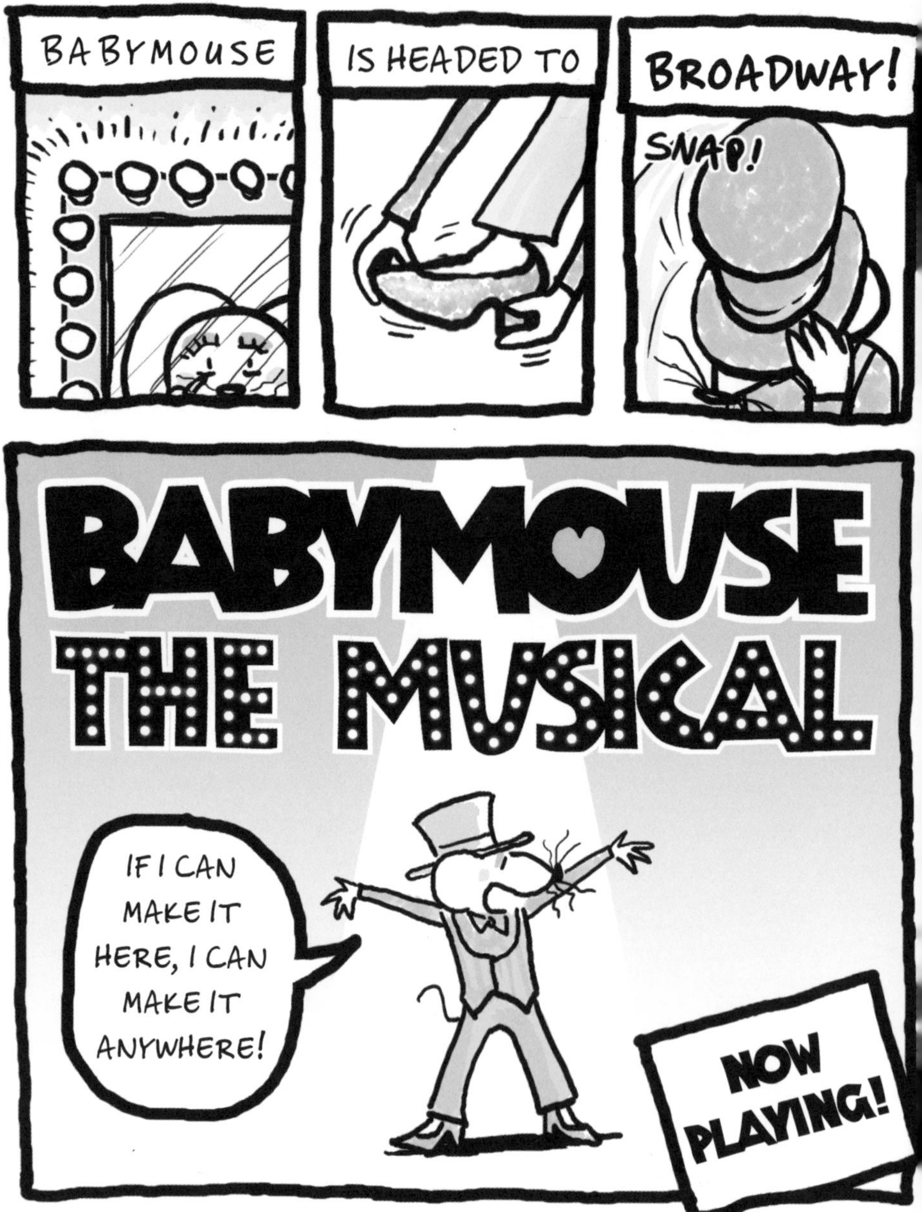
BABYMOUSE
IS HEADED TO
BROADWAY!
SNAP!
BABYMOUSE
THE MUSICAL
IF I CAN MAKE IT HERE, I CAN MAKE IT ANYWHERE!
NOW PLAYING!

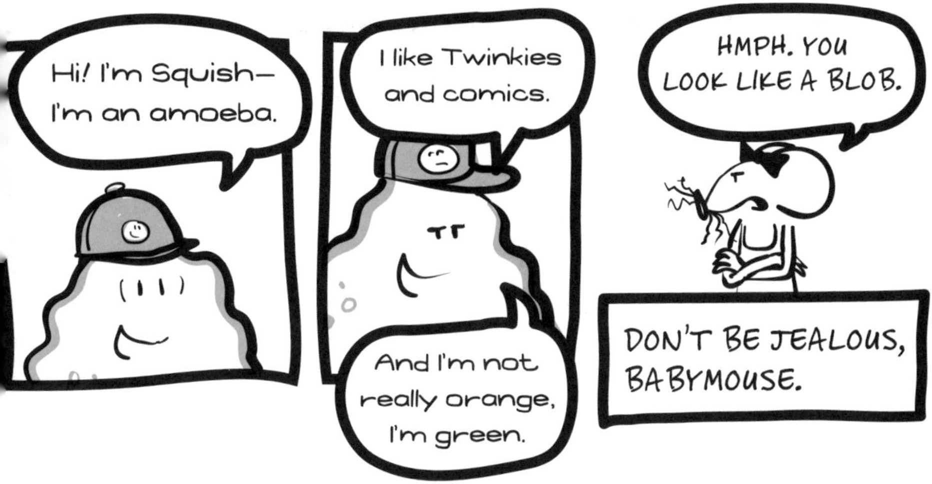
Hi! I'm Squish—
I'm an amoeba.
I like Twinkies and comics.
And I'm not really orange, I'm green.
HMPH. YOU LOOK LIKE A BLOB.
DON'T BE JEALOUS, BABYMOUSE.

READ ABOUT SQUISH'S AMAZING ADVENTURES IN:

#1 SQUISH: Super Amoeba

#2 SQUISH: Brave New Pond

#3 SQUISH: The Power of the Parasite

#4 SQUISH: Captain Disaster

#5 SQUISH: Game On!

AND COMING SOON:

#6 SQUISH: Fear the Amoeba

★ "IF EVER A NEW SERIES DESERVED TO GO VIRAL, THIS ONE DOES."
—*KIRKUS REVIEWS*, STARRED

If you like Babymouse,
you'll love these other great books
by Jennifer L. Holm!

THE BOSTON JANE TRILOGY
EIGHTH GRADE IS MAKING ME SICK
MIDDLE SCHOOL IS WORSE THAN MEATLOAF
OUR ONLY MAY AMELIA
PENNY FROM HEAVEN
TURTLE IN PARADISE

THEY'RE REALLY GOOD! TRUST ME!